'It's terrible what you milkmen do to get business,' she says, squirting another load of foaming suds into the bath. 'You stop at nothing, do you?'

I don't answer her at once because it had never occurred to me that there was a business angle to what I am doing — or about to do. . . . There was I, feeling a bit guilty about being on the job when I should be on the job, and all the time I *am* on the job . . . with this happy thought bubbling through my mind I step forward briskly. . . .

Also by Timothy Lea

CONFESSIONS OF A POP PERFORMER
CONFESSIONS FROM A HEALTH FARM
CONFESSIONS FROM THE SHOP FLOOR
CONFESSIONS OF A LONG DISTANCE LORRY DRIVER
CONFESSIONS OF A PLUMBER'S MATE
CONFESSIONS OF A PRIVATE DICK
CONFESSIONS FROM A LUXURY LINER
CONFESSIONS FROM A NUDIST COLONY

Timothy Lea

Confessions of a Milkman

Futura Publications Limited
A Futura Book

A Futura Book

First published in Great Britain in 1976
by Futura Publications Limited

Copyright © World Publishing Co Est 1976

ISBN 0 8600 7404 8

Printed in Great Britain by
Hazell Watson & Viney Ltd
Aylesbury, Bucks

Futura Publications Limited
110 Warner Road, Camberwell
London SE5

CONTENTS

Chapter One

In which Timmy has a disturbing dream sparked off by his new profession.

Chapter Two

In which Timmy begins to get the hang of his new job under guidance of fellow milkman, Fred Glossop, and obliging customer, Mrs. Nyrene Gadney.

Chapter Three

In which brother-in-law, Sidney Noggett, expresses an oblique interest in becoming a milkman.

Chapter Four

In which Timmy goes on a course and has his eyes opened by well-stacked instructoress, Betty Tromble.

Chapter Five

In which Timmy gets to grips with Mrs. Farley who has got a bit behind – she has not been paying her bills either.

Chapter Six

In which Timmy becomes involved with Sue Dangerfield of the Milk Marketing Board and a dissatisfied customer.

Chapter Seven

In which Sid gets an idea of how to make a bit on the side and Timmy's girlfriend is got at.

Chapter Eight

In which Timmy is taken out of himself in unusual circumstances by a lady called Hermione.

Chapter Nine

In which Timmy becomes sucked into the vortex of the Balham Self Service Society and gets involved in an unusual competition.

Chapter Ten

In which Timmy is interrupted whilst getting to grips with a new customer.

Chapter Eleven

In which Timmy and Sid take Daisy to the Festival of Milk.

CHAPTER ONE

In which Timmy has a disturbing dream sparked off by his
new profession.

What I can't understand is why all the taps in the bath
are shaped like Sid's mug. I mean, if he was sticking
over the side of a church with water pouring out of his
cakehole like one of those gargles I would not be surprised – but a gold tap! If you are going to mess about
with gold you want to do something nice with it, don't
you? Anyway, I haven't got time to worry about that.
Not with all the young maidens bearing pitchers of ass's
milk and emptying them into the bath – don't ask me
how I know it is ass's milk. It just feels like it. Fresh
from the ass too, I should reckon, because it is quite
warm.

Some of these birds are fantastic. Naked to the waist
– going downwards, of course – and slim as England's
chances in the next World Cup. They are of what you
might call dusky hue and their knockers dangle temptingly like inverted foxgloves. I can imagine how they feel;
soft and silky, satisfyingly full . . . Steady Lea! Control
yourself.

The bath is beginning to fill up fast now – and not
just with ass's milk. The girls empty their pitchers and
then get in the bath. I suppose it helps to raise the milk
level but it does seem a bit unusual. Still the line of girls
stretches back out beyond the marble pillars and disap-

pears through the wrought-iron gates so there should be no shortage of supply. Those loin cloths are attractive. Simple and so easy to release. You just tug the knob at the waist and – ooh! That was a bit cheeky. Perhaps she tugged the wrong knob by mistake. But no! She's done it again. What lovely eyes she has. And that smile. Revealing Teds as white as the milk that is now lapping round our navels. Her barnet is held in place by one of those little caps like they wear in Joe Lyons and, now I come to think of it, she is a dead ringer for the bird who sold me the Cornish pasty at dinner time. Still, she couldn't be. How would she get from Joe Lyons to the Sultan's harem in just a few hours? There was a swarthy geezer behind me in the queue but I only heard him ask for a couple of doughnuts – ooh! She's done it again. This must be love. Either that or the bath is so full of crumpet that you can't help bumping into it. And still the line of vase-carrying beauties stretches away into the distance. I suppose that is what they mean out here when they talk about 'going to the pitchers'. Oh! Now there is another of them at it. It's a good job that ass's milk is not transparent otherwise it might be embarrassing. Aaarh. What a soft, beautiful mouth. It seems to have appeared from nowhere and is now browsing on my lips. Tingles run through my system and I feel myself growing, growing . . . blimey! Is that me? That huge tutti-frutti all rooty with the birds nibbling it like they are playing a giant flute? It cannot be true. Soaring out of the milk it is like a nuclear sub breaking through the icecap. And the sensations! And all those lovely girls pressed against me! Oh, it's too much, it really is. I don't think I'll be able to hold on much – Wait a minute! Who's the geezer with the scimitar and the baggy trousers? The turban with the cockade and the mean expression on his mug? Why is he wading through the milk towards me. 'Sid!' I shout the word but no sound comes out of my mouth. I try to move but the weight of birds on top of me makes it impossible. Only my enormous hampton trembles in the slipstream of Sid swinging back his sword. 'No!!' Again, not a sound. Sid's features set in an evil smile and the muscles in his arms tighten. 'You can't!' I am using every ounce of strength I possess but not moving an inch. It is as if I have been drugged, as if I am standing outside myself trying to get back in. 'Whooosh!' "Yaaaaaaargh!!!" I am so relieved to hear the sound of my own voice shouting into the night that I nearly shout again. Night! A second wave of relief arrives almost simultaneously with the first. I have been dreaming. Clammy and half strangled by sheets, I shake myself free and listen to a distant train. 17, Scraggs Lane seems quiet as a grave – which it resembles in many ways. I wonder if I have woken Mum and Dad? Contrary to what one might think, Dad is a light sleeper. He gets so much kip at the lost property office where he works and in front of the telly that he is quite perky during the time the rest of the world gets its head down.

I listen to the silence and then pull the bedclothes about me. What a bleeding nasty dream. If there are going to be any more like that I don't fancy going back to kip. Just to be on the safe side I check that the old action man kit is still joined to the rest of me. Phew! What a relief. You never quite know with dreams, do you? Maybe it – no. For a moment I had hoped that it might have retained some of the lustrous promise of the harem but it seems very ordinary at the moment. Very, very ordinary. Still, better to have it intact and in working order than miniaturized by my brother-in-law's scimitar. Funny him turning up like that. It is probably very symbolic. I believe that Clement Freud has done a lot of work in this area when not flogging dog food for the Liberal Party. He says that everything you dream has a meaning. I wonder what meaning having your hampton cut off by your brother-in-law has? Probably not a very nice one. I suppose I could write to Mr Freud about it but it does seem a bit delicate and the Liberals have enough problems of that kind as it is, don't they? Better to save the cost of the postage stamp and buy a controlling interest in British Leyland.

It is funny about the milk though. I mean, coming so soon after my interview at the depot. I suppose I must be keyed up at the thought of going out on the rounds with Mr Glossop. Two weeks with him, a week's course, and I could have my own float. A steady income, regular hours and virtually your own boss. It can't be bad, can it? And no Sid. I have been tagging along under his thumb for too long. All his crackpot schemes have got me nowhere. I have been exploited. I feel myself going hot under the pyjama collar and take a couple of long, deep breaths. Cool it, Lea. Sid is not going to like it but there is nothing he can do. If you want to be a milk-man that is your decision.

Cupping my hands round my goolies just in case Sid and his scimitar are within swinging distance, I prepare myself for the big day.

CHAPTER TWO

In which Timmy begins to get the hang of his new job under guidance of fellow milkman, Fred Glossop, and obliging customer, Mrs. Nyrene Gadney.

'You can imagine how I feel,' says Fred Glossop. 'Twenty years, that's a long time.'

I rub my hands together and nod. I know how I feel: bleeding parky. And we have only just left the depot. Still, it is only six o'clock and it must get warmer – lighter, too.

'Are you tired, lad?'

I swallow my yawn and try and look like I am just waiting to come out the traps at Harringay. 'I didn't sleep very well last night. I was a bit keyed up. You know what it's like when you want to be certain to wake up. You always wake up an hour earlier.'

Fred nods, showing neither interest nor sympathy. 'If you can't get yourself up in the morning you might as well forget about the job. I've never found it a problem myself.'

Fred Glossop must be about sixty and looks as if he has never heard anything but bad news all his life. You only have to start a sentence and he is nodding pessimistically before you have got further than 'it's a pity – '.

'It's going to be a bit of a problem when you retire,' I say, listening to the whine of the float as we whirr past the lines of parked cars.

'Oh no, not at all,' says Fred – he disagrees with everything you say, as well. 'I've always been able to amuse myself. My mind's always on the go. That's vital when you work by yourself. If you haven't got an active mind you might as well forget it.'

'Um, yes,' I say. 'This thing easy to drive, is it?'

An expression almost of horror arrives on Fred's face. 'You're not going to drive it,' he says looking towards the pavement as if hoping to find someone to share his amazement with. 'Not yet. These are specialized vehicles, you know.'

'It's only a bloody great battery, isn't it?' I say, beginnig to feel a bit choked. 'I don't want to enter it for a Grand Prix.'

When you arrive at the depot in the morning all the battery-operated floats are on charge. The leads stretch away like mechanical milkers fastened to a cow's udder. It is all very symbolic.

'There's no need for that tone,' reprimands Fred. 'After twenty years I ought to know the regulations. We'll put you through your paces at the depot. You could be cut to pieces out here – look at that one!' A car pulls out of the line in front of us without giving a signal and I catch a glimpse of a dry-faced man using an electric shaver with one hand while he drives with the other.

'Off to the office?' I say.

'Or home,' says Fred making a 'tch, tch' noise. 'There's a lot of it goes on round here. People's moral values seem to have plummeted.'

'You must have seen a lot of changes,' I say. This remark is always guaranteed to give any boring old fart over the age of thirty-five enough to talk about for the rest of his life and Fred Glossop is no exception.

'There's no comparison,' he says. 'There's not many of the old ones left. All these people coming in from outside have changed the whole character of the community. Look at that. Wire baskets of flowers hanging in the porch. I ask you! Of course, the kids from the Alderman Wickham Estate come and nick them.' A certain grim satisfaction enters his voice and then fades quickly. 'Still, they're horrible little baskets themselves. Where are you from?'

I am not quite certain I care for the way he moves smoothly from talk of 'horrible little baskets' to an enquiry after my place of residence but I let the matter pass. 'Scraggs Lane,' I say.

'Oh.' Glossop sounds surprised. 'You're local then.' His tone warms on learning that I am not a light-skinned Jamaican. 'That hasn't changed much, has it? Apart from the bits they've pulled down. The wife's mother used to live there until they put her in a flat.' He makes it sound like a cage – quite accurate really. Most of the flats do look like nesting boxes for mice. 'Mrs Summers?'

I shake my head. 'I expect my Mum knows her. Are you going to live round here when you retire?'

Glossop screws up his face like I have slipped a spoonful of cough mixture into his cakehole. 'Worthing,' he says. 'Nice little bungalow. Near enough the front but not so you get the weather and the people. Know what I mean?'

I give him a 'sort of' kind of nod and wrap my arms round my body so that I can tuck my hands under my armpits. Gawd but it is taters. I can see why Fred Glossop wears mittens round his blue, bony fingers.

'Cold, lad?' he says glancing at me disparagingly. 'This isn't cold. Not compared with what it can be. If you find this cold – '

'I'd better forget about the job. Yeah, I know,' I say, finishing his sentence for him and wondering if I am going to be able to stand two weeks with such a miserable old sod. 'How much longer before we get where we're going.'

Glossop looks at me coldly and mutters something under his breath. 'Just round the corner. Up Clyde Avenue, along Barton Way, The Estate, Clark Street, Thurleigh Avenue, south side of the common and back down Nightingale Road.'

'Blimey,' I say. 'All human life is here.'

Glossop gives me a second helping of the freezing glances laced with a deep sigh and slams on the anchors. Our glorious progress is arrested and the crates of milk in the back make 'tut, tut' noises. 'After a while you know what everybody has,' he says. 'It comes automatic. You'll have to look in the book at first. When I collect the divis, that's when I indulge in the sales chat. If a lady's in a delicate condition for instance.'

'You mean if she's broken something?' I say.

The red veins that run across Glossop's face like a map of the world's airlines leak some colour into his hollow cheeks 'I mean, if she's with child.'

'Oh, I get it,' I say. 'When they're in the pudding club you wack in with an extra pint?'

Glossop closes his eyes and nearly drops a couple of

pints of homogenised. 'Don't be disgusting!' he says. 'You'll never get anywhere if you talk like that. You have to present yourself to the public as a fount of practical knowledge and guidance on all matters relating to the beneficial properties of milk and its allied products. They have to respect you.'

'Of course,' I say. 'I quite see that.'

What I am really clocking is the little darling leaning out of the bay window of what must be the sitting room. She is wearing a black halter neck nightie and although her hair has been piled up on top of her head it is starting to tumble down temptingly.

'Sweet little tits,' says Glossop.

'Not so little, either,' I say.

Glossop switches his gaze from the bird table and I realize that there has been a misunderstanding, The judy tosses her head sulkily and closes the window. 'You'll have to watch your step,' says Glossop. 'I can't see you lasting long at this rate.'

By eleven o'clock I am prepared to agree with him. My fingers feel as if they are going to drop off with the cold and I am knackered after struggling up and down hundreds of flights of stairs. I never knew there were so many flat developments. The biggest of them all is the Alderman Wickham Estate and that is where Fred Glossop looks at his watch and strokes his chin thoughtfully. 'Um,' he says. 'I'm going to leave you here for a bit. I want to get something for the wife.'

'How much do you think she's worth?' I ask.

Fred ignores my merry quip and makes off in the direction of the The Nightingale. It occurs to me that his ruddy conk may well be the result of drinking something a good deal stronger than milk. Boozers are often miserable old sods.

The Alderman Wickham Estate is a series of grey skyscrapers and concrete corridors which have very nasty niffs in them. Most of the lifts and rubbish chutes are out of order and the walls exist to show that there are some people who can't even spell four-letter words. Cardboard boxes full of rubbish fall apart in every corner and I can see why Fred Glossop decided to take a powder.

I grab a crate of milk and the order book and head for the lift in Block F. It is out of order. That is no great surprise and I am heading for the stairs when I happen to glance back towards the float. A teeny tea leaf is in the process of half inching a couple of pints of ivory nectar. 'Hey you!' I bellow. I expect the little sod to put the stuff back but he darts across the tarmac still clinging to his swag. I do not hang about because Fred has explained that you get lumbered for any stocks that are lost or mislaid.

'Come back here!' I drop the crate and set off in pursuit like my whole future depends on it – which it might well do. I can't see Fred taking kindly to any deductions from his last pay packet. The kid flashes up a flight of stairs and I am gaining fast when a plastic dustbin bounces down towards me and catches me just below the knees. The little perisher obviously fancies himself as James Bond. I pick myself up and come round the bend in the stairs just fast enough to see him taking off down a corridor. He stops outside the third door, and tries to open it. The door is locked. I allow myself a satisfied smile and begin to saunter down the corridor. A quick clip round the earholes and justice will be done. The kid tucks one of the bottles under his arm and reaches up to ring the doorbell. He is looking dead worried and his finger is pressed against the bell like it has become stuck to it.

'All right, short arse,' I say. 'Hand them over.' I step forward purposefully just as the door opens. A naked woman with dripping glistening boobs cops a pint in each hand. It would make a good advertisement really. The naked knockers and the milk. All together in the all together so to speak. It makes me wish I had drunk more of the stuff when I was a kid. About the age of the little bastard who is now scarpering back down the balcony.

'What do you want?' says the bint, retiring behind the door. 'Haven't you ever seen a woman before?'

'I'm not certain,' I say. 'I thought I had but you make me have second thoughts. I reckon some of the others must have been blokes in drag.'

'If that's a compliment, thank you,' says the bird. 'Now piss off.'

She tries to close the door but I put my foot in it – something I do quite often. 'Excuse me,' I say. 'But that's my milk you're holding.'

It sounds a bit funny when I say it and the woman gives me an old-fashioned look in the area of the all the best. 'As long as it tastes the same as the cow's,' she says.

'Your kiddy nicked it off the float,' I say, allowing an edge of impatience to creep into my voice. 'If you don't give us it back there could be trouble.'

'You're not our milkman,' says the bird showing no sign of handing over the milk.

'I'm helping Mr Glossop,' I say. The bird's face does not register recognition. 'Meadowfresh,' I prompt.

The woman shakes her head. 'I'm with Universal,' she says. 'I'm quite satisfied.' She gives a funny little smile when she says that and I wonder what she means. Because I have a mind like that it occurs to me that she may not be referring only to the practical guidance on the beneficial properties of milk and all the guff so dear to Fred Glossop's heart.

'You may be satisfied but I'm not,' I say. 'Your little boy has just knocked off two pints of Meadowfresh milk.'

'I never saw the child before in my life,' says the bird. 'You want to be careful the things you say. Why don't you go away and stop plaguing people? Do you know how much it costs to heat bath water these days?'

'About the price of a couple of pints of milk, I should think,' I say. 'Now, hand them over please. I don't want to have to get nasty. I saw him taking them off the float with my own eyes.'

I start to push forward but the bird throws her weight against the door. 'I know who you are,' she says. 'You're the one who's been going round rattling the knocker flaps.'

'Don't be ridiculous,' I say. 'I'm a milkman!' I get a bit narked at that point and give the Rory a vicious shove. It flies back and the bird drops one of the milk bottles which shatters on the floor. The carpet is soaked and pieces of glass fly everywhere. The bird lets out a cry of pain and irritation and I immediately felt guilty.

'I'm sorry,' I say. 'I didn't mean to do that.'

'I should hope not,' says the bird. She is trying to cover up her very obvious charms with a couple of arms and the remaining milk bottle and I feel that I ought to do something to make amends.

'Where's the kitchen?' I say. 'I'll get a rag and clean it up.'

'I should bloody well think so,' says the bird. 'If it wasn't for the neighbours I'd call the police. Barging in here like some rapist. You don't come from Cambridge, do you?'

Despite the way the bird is going on at me I can't help feeling that she is well able to look after herself. She has a big pouting mouth and her lower lip sticks forward aggressively like it is trying to upper cut the end of her hooter. She is not tall but very curvy in all the places you would first look if checking her for smuggling hot water bottles. I rather fancy her bristling with anger – or perhaps I should say bristoling.

'I'm on probation,' I say, deciding to try and defuse the situation with a little chat.

'That's reassuring,' says the bird over her shoulder as she disappears into the bathroom.

'I mean I'm having a trial,' I say.

'My old man always went on probation after the trial,' says the bint reappearing in a lilac-covered frilly housecoat. 'Then they got his number and threw him in the nick.'

'A trial as a milkman,' I say. 'That's why I was a bit up tight about the milk. I don't want to put my foot in it.'

'You just have,' says the bird. 'Gawd, you're a clumsy custard, aren't you? Don't wipe it on the carpet!'

'If you give me a rag—'

'You'll make even more of a mess. I'll do it. You pick up the pieces of glass.'

It is funny but it is much more sexy now that she has the housecoat on. All pink and visible she was a bit over-powering. Especially with me wearing my these and those. I don't mind being in the buff with a chick – in fact, I have been known to quite like it – but I never reckon it when one of us is standing there with all the clobber on and the other is as naked as a Tory Party Election manifesto. I can't really think why. It just doesn't seem natural.

'Where's your old man now?' I ask.

'I told you,' she says. 'In the nick.'

We are both kneeling down now and could post a letter in the gap between her knockers – mind you, it wouldn't get very far even if the postman enjoyed open-ing the box.

'You must be lonely,' I say.

'I don't miss him,' she says. 'Thieving was the only thing he was good at – and he wasn't very good at that, was he?'

'I suppose not,' I say. I am so busy looking at her knockers that I jab my finger against a bit of glass and cut it. 'Ouch!'

'I read you for a cack-handed twit the moment you came through the door,' says the bird without great warmth. 'Don't drip all over the carpet! Blimey, come in the bathroom.' She shoves my finger under the cold tap and rummages in the medicine cabinet. 'Blast! There's never one there when you want it.'

'You play with those rubber ducks, do you?' I say, looking at the tray across the bath.

'Don't be daft. They're the—' The bird breaks off and waves a finger at me. 'Oh, cleversticks, eh? Trying to get back to your bleeding milk, are you? Listen, my kiddy would never take anything that didn't belong to him.'

'As opposed to his old man,' I say.

'That's a nasty thing to say,' says the bird striking a pose with her hands on her hips. 'And me helping you out, too. I'd ask you to withdraw that remark. You're the one who's come barging in here without foundation.'

I nearly laugh when she talks about foundations because she could really do with one. She looks like the kind of woman who Marjorie Proops would take in hand and help to get the best out of herself. Mind you, I would not climb over her to get to Cyril Smith. She is quite handsome if you go for gentle curves – especially with the front of her housecoat drifting open and a hint of furry knoll revealing itself. The lady follows my eyes and draws her gown haughtily around her.

'Cheeky bastard,' she says. 'What are you looking at?'

'Your bath water's getting cold,' I say, sticking my finger in it.

'Don't do that! I don't want your bloody finger in it!' She springs forwards and grabs hold of my arm and there we are – touching each other in half a dozen different places at the same time, heaving, breathing – it is like an old Charlton Heston religious epic.

'Hop in and I'll scrub your back,' I say.

The bird looks into my eyes and I hold my breath whilst continuing breathing. 'You'd look,' she says.

I shake my head. 'Not so you'd notice.'

'Keep your bleeding finger out of it.'

'There must be an answer to that,' I say.

But she isn't listening. She slips out of her robe, chucks

it over my head, and by the time I have taken it off she is in the bath, leaning forward so that her bristols are brushing against her knees – that's something Wedgwood Benn can't do. 'All right,' she says. 'The soap's behind you.' She is right too. I grab hold of it and work up a nice rich lather. Cor, can't be bad, can it? I knew there must be more to this milkman business than complaining about the empties not being washed out properly. I kneel down beside the bath and apply my Germans to the lady's I'm alright. (I'm all right, Jack: Back; Ed) Oh dear. The moment I feel the soft, warm flesh, Percy gets an attack of the space probes. How untoward of him. I am trying to break the tension between myself and this Richard, and the old groin greyhound has to introduce another fifteen and a half centimetres of it – note: a metric-mad mick makes for more majestic mating, men.

'Is that all right?' I say.

'I've known worse,' say the bird. 'Did you ever use to clean windows?'

'Yes I did,' I say. 'That's amazing! How did you know?'

'Because you've practically pushed a couple of panes out of the middle of my back! Go a bit easy, will you?'

'It's the effect you have on me,' I say. 'I'm trying to be gentle but something about you excites my blood.'

'Blimey!' says the judy. 'You've seen too much telly, haven't you? Where did you learn to talk like that?'

'It comes naturally,' I say modestly.

'Uum. Not the only thing I should think. I'm not surprised you've dropped the soap – OOH!'

'Sorry,' I say. 'It slipped.'

'It didn't slip there, there isn't room for it! Mind what you're doing!'

'Perhaps I'd better try the other side,' I say.

'You don't mind, do you?' she says.

'Not if you don't.' I wack off another handful of lather and slap it onto her knockers – well, not so much slap as get it on before she can complain too loudly. Not that she does complain too loudly – in fact, she doesn't complain at all. Her nipples turn to large acorns beneath my fingers and she closes her eyes and shivers.

'Ooh!' she says. 'I bet you're going to drop it again.' A hint is seldom lost on the toast of the Clapham south side crumpet thrashers and I watch the large pink lump bump down the curve of her Ned Kelly. Another large pink lump is coming up from the other direction – though outside the bath. Yes! – percy is making the front of my trousers a lousy place to store a bunch of bananas. My hand follows the soap down below the water line and loses interest in it immediately. Something soft and slippery welcomes my inquisitive fingers and experience suggests that it is not an empty banana skin.

'AAAAaargh!' I was expecting a reaction but nothing quite so violent. Hardly have I sent my digits motoring up down passion alley than the lady grabs me and nearly hauls me into the bath with her. I wonder how long her old man has been in the nick? I hope he doesn't choose this morning to come back on parole. There is enough blood on the carpet as it is. 'I'm making your shirt all wet aren't I?'

'Well – er yes, I suppose you – maybe I'd better take it – yes!'

It doesn't take you long to get the drift with this lady. Once she has decided that she likes you she doesn't send messages in code. She helps me off with my shirt and three of its buttons and if I did not stand against the wall to take off my trousers she would have the zip out of them as well.

'It's terrible what you milkmen do to get business,' she says squirting another load of foaming suds into the bath. 'You stop at nothing, do you?'

I don't answer her at once because it had never occurred to me that there was a business angle to what I am doing – or about to do. It goes right back to Sid's golden maxim when we were cleaning windows – keep the customer satisfied. There was I, feeling a bit guilty about being on the job when I should be on the job, and all the time I *am* on the job. If this little session is going to help me wrestle a customer from Universal it is well worth while apart from any pleasure given and received along the way. With this happy thought bubbling through my mind I step forward briskly and discover that my hostess has two bars of soap. One in the bath and the other the one I stand on before breaking a new record for aquatic muff dives.

'Oh, you impetuous fool!' she says, as I raise my dripping nut from between her legs.

'How do you hold your breath down there?' And before I can answer she has shoved my crust down again.

'Madam, please!' I say, struggling to the surface. 'Are you trying to kill me?'

'What a way to go,' she says.

'For you, maybe,' I say. 'I have plans to die in bed.'

'We'll try the bed later,' says the woman, hardly pausing for breath. 'Come here, it's lovely when we're all slippery together.'

She does not hang about but shoves her arms round me and hugs me to her Bristols – definitely First Division material. She lies back and another couple of gallons of water slop on to the floor. Honestly, you should see the place. It is like the fountains in Trafalgar Square – though without the bloody pigeons, thank God. Water is still dripping off the ceiling from when I dived into the bath and the floor is awash. Still, that is not my problem. Once again, I am succumbing to my sensitive nature. Think of Meadowfresh, Lea. Think of this lovely lady's snatch wriggling enticingly against the tip of your hampton. Yes, I think I prefer the second inducement. My playmate can't use a water softener because my tonk is more rigid than a tungsten steel tuning fork. I lunge through the H_2O and clobber the clam first go. Dead centre – you can always tell because you don't meet anything until your balls bang into each other as they lock shoulders in the entrance to the love shaft.

'Ewwwgh!' Forgive me if I have spelt it wrong but it sounds a bit like that. The contented expulsion of air from the throat of the owner of a barbecued Berkeley. Another tidal wave hits the floor and I get enough suds up my hooter to wash Idi Amin's smalls for a week – well, half a week. Wishing that I had knees with small rubber suckers attached to them, I try and achieve some purchase against the bottom – excuse that word – of the bath. My new friend has wrapped her legs round me and I reckon she could crack boulder-sized walnuts if she put her mind to it – which in the position she is adopting would be quite an achievement. Honestly, I find the whole performance – and the hole performance, too – very difficult. I read in a book once about this couple having it off in the bath and floating glasses of champagne backwards and forwards between each other but I don't see how they could have done it. The only way I can screw this judy satisfactorily is with her head under the water and this can't be very nice for her after the first five minutes.

'Let's get on the floor,' she says.

'Good idea,' I say. 'That's where most of the bath water is.' I am not kidding. One of the rubber ducks has floated across the room and is bumping against the door like it is trying to peck a hole in it.

'Who's a nice clean boy?' says the bird as we flop on to the floor. 'I could eat my dinner off you, couldn't I?' Without more ado she drops her nut and starts on the first course. Very arresting it is too. I reckon she would have a water ice down to the stick in about thirty-five seconds. Not that I am grumbling. I would rather have her lips round my hampton than a swarm of bees any day of the week.

'Ooh!' I say. 'Ah! No! Don't – don't – don't – DON'T STOP!'

'You're sex-mad,' she says, looking up from my gleaming knob. 'You're an animal, aren't you?'

'Do you like animals?' I say.

'Ye-es' says the lady and she starts again.

O-o-o-o-o-o-o-H! Talk about thrills running up and down your spine. Mine are travelling by motor bike – and I wish my old man was wearing a crash helmet. If she goes on like this much longer there is going to be a nasty accident. O-o-oh! Another few seconds and she stands to cop the cream off the top of my bottle. This cannot be in the best interest of ultimate client satisfaction and my astute business brain wakes up to its responsibilities. Removing my dick from the lady's cakehole – it is rather like trying to take a bone away from your pet pooch – I measure the bird's length against the slippery lino – five foot two and eyes of blue – and give her rose hips a gentle going over with my brewer's bung. She is clearly not averse to this treatment and squeezes my hampton like it is one of those gadgets for strengthening your grip.

'Ooh,' she says. 'I know what would be nice now.'

A few years ago I might have thought she was talking about a cup of tea but wise men find time an instructive mistress (good that bit, isn't it? Gives the whole narrative a touch of class) and I have a pretty clear idea what she is getting at – or rather what she would like me to be getting at – a touch of the old cunning linctus, or whatever they call it. I know it sounds like a cough mixture – and you can need some of it if you get a few hairs wound round your epiglotis. Anyway, I have got to be nice to her if I want to convert her to Meadowfresh and after a nifty muff dive she should be putty in my hands. No point in throwing it away too lightly though. I might as well weigh in with a bit of sales chat. I expect Fred Glossop would in my situation – though, come to think of it, I can't really see Fred Glossop in my situation.

'Oh yes!' I breathe passionately. 'Yes, yes, yes!' Notice the clever way I get her thinking in terms of the affirmative. She is practically nodding as I close my Teds gently round her strawberry ripples. 'Have you ever thought of changing?'

She raises her head slightly. 'You mean, being a fellow?' Fortunately I stop myself from grinding my teeth together.

'No!' I say. 'I mean, no. I was talking about changing your dairy. Meadowfresh has got a lot to offer.' I drop my nut down to her tummy button and start eel-darting my tongue into the dainty little dip.

'Oh yes?' she gasps. 'Ooh.'

'I was wondering if you would be interested?' I say. 'You could keep the milt – I mean, the milk – as a free sample. I think you'll notice the difference. Rich, creamy . . .'

I get my tongue down till it is nearly part of the pattern on the lino and bring it up slowly.

'Oh, oh, OH!' The lady's backside lifts off the floor like my tongue has the power of levitation.

'Would you like me to give it a try?'

Her hands go into my barnet and for a moment I wonder if she has Red Indian blood. 'Oh yes!' she says. 'Yes! Yes!!'

What a satisfying moment. A contented customer and she hasn't even tried the product yet. This must be my best ever start at any job.

I give her dilly pot a few more tongue tickles and then reckon that the time is favourable to give Percy his head – well, he has had her head, hasn't he? Rising to my shapely knees I prepare to drive proud perce home—and I don't mean back to 17, Scraggs Lane, ancestral home of the Leas. As it turns out this task is unnecesary because Meadowfresh's latest recruit has her greedy mits round it like she fears it might disappear if exposed to the light. With the speed of British Leyland going on strike

28

she has whipped my action man kit into her snatch and clamped her ankles over mine. 'Wheeh-ouch!' Unfortunately her bum catches on a ridge where the lino is breaking up but the floor is so slippery that we don't stay in one place for long. I try and brace my legs against the door, but end up sliding the length of the room and nearly fracturing my nut against the washbasin holders.

'This is no good,' I say. 'Come on!' I sit on the edge of the bath and the bird is on to my lap like your moggy on to Dad's favourite armchair. The aim is what you might call unerring. I bet she is a minor miracle at quoits.

'Ooh,' she says. 'This is the third time I've come. Do you do deliveries on Sundays? That's when Edwin goes to his Gran.'

'Not every Sunday,' I say, beginning to calculate that I could be on the way to an early grave if all my new customers appreciate the same line of sales technique. 'Ooh! Ow! Eeh! Ah!'

Fortunately, release in the form of sending a few million sperm cells to a better place and falling backwards into the bath comes to my aid and I am eventually able to limp away with an assurance from Mrs Nyrene Gadney – for that is the lady's name – that it is Universal out and Meadowfresh in! What a triumphant start to my new career. Fred Glossop will be pleased with me. I do not exactly dance but my step is light as I emerge from the staircase and find the man himself standing by the empty milk float. 'Where in the name of the Lord have you been!?' he says.

'Just signed up a new customer, Fred,' I say. 'A Mrs Gadney. Nice lady. I've got her down for—' I break off when I see that Fred is staring at the empty float and shaking. 'I'm sorry,' I say. 'You had to finish the round by yourself, did you? I didn't know it was going to take so long. It took a bit of time to get her interested in my bollocks – I mean, products!'

'You stupid half wit!' shouts Glossop. 'I haven't delivered a drop. While you've been frigging about, the whole bleeding lot has been knicked by kids!'

CHAPTER THREE

In which brother-in-law, Sidney Noggett, expresses an oblique interest in becoming a milkman.

'Pissed off with it yet, are you?' says Sid.

'Course not,' I say. 'It's very interesting. I wish they'd turn the bloody muzak down in this place.'

Sid refuses to be diverted. 'I reckon it's a comedown, myself,' he says. 'You wouldn't catch me trying to flog bleeding yoghurt.'

'They haven't got around to putting blood in it yet.' I say. 'Are you going to buy me a drink? My glass has dried out.'

'A half?' says Sid hopefully.

'Pint, thanks,' I say. 'What are you doing these days?'

'I'm weighing things up,' says Sid.

'On the veg counter at Sainsbury's?'

Sid pats my cheek. 'You're full of fun today, aren't you?' he says. 'How would you fancy a plate of scrambled teeth for dinner? When I say "weighing up" I am referring to a judicious appraisal of the career opportunities currently pissing themselves to get at me.'

'So you're on the sausage,' I say.

Sid sighs. 'How typical,' he says. 'You have difficulty seeing to the end of your hooter, don't you? I don't want to insult the welfare state by not taking what's due to me. Just because I'm public-spirited it doesn't mean that I can't organize my own destiny. I'm not rushing, that's all.' He breaks off and sucks in his breath sharply. 'Cor. She's a bit of all right, isn't she?'

'Yes,' I say. 'Hello Nyrene.'

'You know her?' says Sid.

'She's a customer,' I say, nonchalanly wiping some froth off my hooter with the end of Sid's tie.

'She turned a funny colour when she saw you,' says Sid. 'You given her one, have you?'

'Sid, please,' I say 'A gentleman never discusses things like that. Let's just say we shared something rather beautiful. Afternoon.' I am addressing the girl in the black halter neck nightie I saw on the job with Fred Glossop – I mean, on the round with Fred Glossop. She is wearing a stretch sweater that must have belonged to one of her kid sister's dolls.

'Another customer?' says Sid. He takes a quick, dabbing swig at his beer.

'Yes,' I say. 'Nice kid.'

'Er – what's it like down at the depot?' says Sid, very casual-like.

'Thinking about a job?' I say.

Sid splutters. 'What? You must be joking. Just expressing an interest, that's all. I wouldn't take a job I didn't want just because there was a bit of crumpet going with it. What was she like?'

'Which one?' I say.

'The one with the big knockers. The first one.'

'Nyrene?' I say. 'Well – ' I look round and lower my voice discreetly. 'Would you believe fantastic?'

'Go on,' says Sid.

'That's just what she said,' I tell him. 'Honestly, there

was no holding her. I was frightened for my life once or twice, I don't mind telling you.'

Sid gazes towards the stool on which Nyrene is perching showing a fair amount of Scotch egg. 'She looks a goer,' he says thoughtfully.

'Comes, goes – you name it,' I say. 'I just hope your life insurance payments are up to date. It would be bad enough for Rosie hearing how you snuffed it. I remember when she grabbed my—'

'She's looking this way!' hissed Sid. 'I think she fancies me.'

'Well, sign up then,' I say. 'That way you'll be certain to get a crack at her.

'I don't have to sign up!' says Sid. 'I can pull her just as I am. I don't have to hide my magnetism behind a milk float.'

'Just as you like, Sid,' I say. Frankly, I am a bit knackered after my chava with Mrs Gadney and the excitement of the first day and I don't care what Sid does.

'I'm going to pull her,' says Sid, draining his pint. 'You want to watch this. You're never too old to pick up tips.'

'You've got a bit of pork pie at the corner of your mouth,' I say.

'I was going to give her that for supper,' says Sid. 'Right, stand by for an attack of the old verbal magic.' He tucks his paunch into his trousers and glides across the floor like he is on a monorail. Mrs Gadney has just fished in her bag for a fag and Sid arrives at exactly the right moment to set fire to it. He carries a lighter which he wears in a little leather pouch round his neck and he leans forwards sexily, and gazes moodily into Mrs

Gadney's eyes. It is a pity he does not look towards the fag because he would see that his tie is draped over the top of the lighter. He presses the plunger and I can smell the scorched fibres from where I am sitting. Oh dear, what a shame. Sid always fancied that tie, too. Anyway, it gets him into conversation with Nyrene and I suppose that is the main thing.

I am just wandering up to join them when the door flies open and a bloke comes in who commands attention. He is about six foot four with a thick tash and hands that hang so low they brush against his knees. He is slightly less wide than the Oval gasometer and if he has a smile he must have given it the evening off. It is not difficult to guess at his profession because he is wearing a striped apron and has a peaked cap tipped on the back of his head. The badge on the cap says UD and you don't have to have 'A' Levels to know that stands for Universal Dairies. I suppose his arms must have lengthened after years of humping milk crates about. Either that or his mum was having it off with a gorilla. He looks round the room and when he sees Nyrene and Sid he gives a little shiver. Something about the gesture makes me slow down my progress towards Clapham's answer to Paul Newman and I burrow into the crowd round the bar.

'What's this then?' says the big Herbert waving a piece of paper under Nyrene's nose.

Everybody looks round and Nyrene flushes a shade darker, 'It's what it says,' pouts Nyrene. 'I've decided to change. You were collecting empties late this evening, weren't you?'

'I came to see you!' growls the bloke.

'Well, that's as maybe,' says Nyrene. 'I've got fixed up elsewhere.' She looks down the bar towards where she last saw me and I duck down so low that a bloke thinks I am trying to sup out of his pint. 'Meadowsweet,' says Nyrene.

'Fresh,' says Sid. 'Meadowfresh.'

The bloke who has been staring at Nyrene slowly transfers his attention to Sid. It is like peeling chewing gum off moquette. 'What did you say?' he asks.

'Meadowfresh,' says Sid all helpful like. 'The name of the firm is Meadowfresh. M – E – A – ' Sid falters when he sees the way the bloke is looking at him. ' – D – O – ' The barman sweeps a handful of glasses beneath the bar. ' – W. That's one word. F – R – '

'So! You're trying to take the piss as well as my girl,' says the geezer menacingly.

'No!' says Sid, wising up to danger. 'You've got it all wrong. It's not me it's – ' WHUUUUMP!! I never thought it was possible to uppercut someone so that they could hop on to a bar but Sid goes up into the air like his jaw is glued to the end of the guy's fist. 'Wait a minute!' he squeals. 'You've got it all wrong. It's not me you want it's – ' WAMP!!

I must say, I do like this fellow's timing. By the time Sid has bounced off the line of stout bottles at the back of the bar and slid down on to a crate of empties he has nothing to say about anything.

'What did you do that for?' squeals Nyrene, clearly annoyed. 'He never did you any harm.'

'Depends what you mean by harm,' says the angry

milkman. He leans over the bar and is trying to grab Sid when the landlord lays him out with a cricket bat. I can see that this milkman business is going to be tougher than I had thought.

CHAPTER FOUR

In which Timmy goes on a course and has his eyes opened by well-stacked instructoress, Betty Tromble.

'Now, let's go right back to where it all starts,' says Miss Tromble. 'The cow. We all know how many stomachs a cow has, don't we?'

I nod, but I am not thinking about a cow's stomach. I am thinking about Miss Tromble's knockers. They move me – well, they move part of me. The bit that frays the inside of my Y-fronts. I have never seen a woman with such enormous bristols. They swell away from her chest like the sails on an ocean schooner running before a hurricane. When she comes round a corner they arrive a couple of minutes before the rest of her. They are beginning to prey on my mind. I can't concentrate on the difference between homogenised and pasteurised milk or how much is lost in unreturned empties every year. All I can do is gaze upon the beginning of the snowy vastness and wonder what the whole lot looks like, feels like, tastes like! There is a loud crackling noise and I realize that in my passion I have squeezed the life out of a blackcurrant yoghurt container. Luckily it is empty. Miss Tromble looks at me coldly. That's the trouble, she always looks at me coldly. She seems to have no awareness of how I feel about her – or would like to feel about her. She seems inexorably wed to her craft, that of a lecturer at Meadowfresh Residential Course for aspiring

37

milkmen – perspiring in my case. It is warm in the lecture room and the Tromble knockers discreetly veiled behind their owner's crisply laundered white coat are making me feverish. I must have a gander at them! I wonder if she is aware of the feelings she gives rise to? I glance round the other blokes on the course: Ted Gunter who took a first in dandruff at Oxford University, Norman Hollis with the leather patches on his elbows and the row of biros in his top pocket, Jim Keen with the beard and the polo neck. They are all watching her knockers like they are hypnotised by them. She must know. Perhaps the breast feature is an embarrassment to her. It must be terrible having blokes like me staring at you all the time. The least I could do is be a bit more discreet about it. I wonder where her room is. It must be somewhere in the buildings. All the staff are residential. When I think about it I get another little shiver to add to the crop down the front of my trousers. I don't usually go much on being a peeping Tom but spying on Miss Tromble as she revealed her super chassis would be a bit special. There is something very haughty and reserved about her that brings out the lusty peasant in me. What the butler saw, that's it. Humble, earthy Timothy Lea watches the lady of the manor stripping down to the buff – 'crack!' Another yoghurt container up the spout.

'Do you mind not doing that?' says the lovely Tromble, coldly. 'Apart from being wasteful it's very distracting.'

'Exactly,' says Gunter on my right. He is a real toffee-nosed berk who takes notes all the time and leaps about opening doors whenever Miss Tromble gets within forty paces. Why he wants to be a milkman, I don't know.

38

I reckon he must have got into a bit of trouble some-where and ended up with the tin tack.

Finding Miss Tromble's room is a cinch because I follow her when she leaves the lecture room and goes up the staircase with 'Staff Only' written at the bottom of it. I give her a couple of seconds to go round the bend – you know what I mean – take a crafty shufti round the entrance hall and scamper up the stairs just in time to see her steering her mighty Manchesters through the second door along the oak-panelled corridor. So, that is where she snuggles down beside them for the night. Just across the way from the milking sheds. Very handy when I come to think of it. There is certain to be a loft above the prize Friesians and I should be able to cop an un-interrupted view of the plus feature if I can find a handy window. I check out the joint during my dinner hour and it could not be better. I can practically see my mug in the mirror on her dressing table. It all depends how tightly she draws her curtains.

I can hardly concentrate on Simple Accounting Pro-cedures and Know Your Way Round Your Float, which takes up most of the afternoon. Gunther, Hollis and Keen are such earnest, dedicated buggers. It makes my heart bleed to see them scribbling away in their little books and smiling up at Miss Tromble like she invented Christ-mas. They would not know what to do with her knockers if they were lowered on to them face downwards from a crane. Gunter especially. What a prick. The old school tie with egg all over it. And the way they all team up together. You would think they had never been away from home before. They really put the mockers on me.

I would not be surprised if there was something a bit unhealthy about their relationship. Latent, of course. They would not have the guts to flash their old men in earnest – or perhaps I should say Ernest, ha! ha! – oh well, please yourselves.

Comes the evening I bolt down my bangers and mash and settle down with an old *Woman* where I can keep an eye on Miss Tromble who is eating daintily on the staff table. We eat in a blooming great room called the refectory which has a few easy chairs and old magazines in one corner of it. Also a ping pong table.

The object of my desires is wearing a kind of lace blouse and I can see the outline of her white bra beneath. I have to confess that she is on the plump side but with a pair of knockers like that everything else would have to be in proportion. If it wasn't she would topple forward every time she stood up.

'Feel like making up a four?' Twit Gunter is standing in front of me with a couple of table tennis bats in his mit. 'Equipment's a bit ropy, I'm afraid, but you can have the bat with the rubber on it.'

'Thanks a zillion,' I say, trying not to sound too sarky. 'It's not my game.'

'We thought we might slip out for a swift half later,' continues Terrible Ted lowering his voice. 'Norman has got a wheeze.'

'You won't find a chemist open at this time of night,' I say wittily. 'No thanks, I think I'll get an early night.'

Miss Tromble has just started the laborious task of brushing the crumbs off her knockers and I know that she will soon rise – like something else not a million miles from the back of my fly. Honestly, Percy has fallen very deeply in love with Miss Tromble and is now trying to show his feelings in a brave attempt at a Hitler salute. I lower the feature on Princess Margaret – 'The little girl who grew up' – on to my lap – hoping that no harm will come to Her Royal Highness by my so doing – and stand up, pressing Percy back against my tum.

'Sure you won't change your mind? You could be in for a spot of fun.' Another thing I can't stand about Gunter is that he is very slow to take a hint.

'No, thanks,' I say. 'I'm going to brush up on my milk grades. Good night.'

I nod to the others and stroll out into the hall. There is a notice board there and I pretend to look at a poster about the local hunter trials whilst I wait for Miss Tromble to emerge. I had always thought that peeping Toms were dirty old men in plastic raincoats, not clean-limbed lads like myself. It just shows you that life is full of surprises, doesn't it?

After a few minutes, Miss Tromble emerges and pauses in the doorway. She looks towards me and her eyes seem to stare right through me. I feel myself blush and turn back to the dates of the hunter trials as if I am trying to memorise them. The way Miss Tromble looked at me you would think that she knew what was on my mind. A questioning, accusing look. What a despicable creature I am when you think about it – even if you don't think about it. Setting out to spy on a woman removing her clothes. What total lack of human decency and moral fibre. How will I ever be able to live with myself if I go through with this vile act? Oh well, I will be able to tell in the morning. At least, I won't have to wait too long.

'Do you fancy a cup of coffee, Betty?'

'No thanks, it keeps me awake.'

'Right, if you hang on a moment, I'll get that book.'

'Thanks, Derek.'

The man talking to Miss Tromble springs off so fast that he nearly splits his cavalry twills. So, the fair temptress is called Betty and has plans for kip. No time to lose. I stroll casually towards the front door and, once through it, hare round the side of the building. There is a light outside the cowshed and I have to go carefully to make sure that no one is watching from the main building as I slip inside. I suppose I could always say I was revising the number of teats on an udder if anyone asked me what I was doing. All the cows are in their stalls and a few heads turn to gaze at me suspiciously. Do I see reproach in those large, brown eyes? Probably not. Cows always look like that. Only one little number seems agitated and she has a calf. She shakes her head from side to side and suddenly lunges forward angrily. There is a snapping noise and her halter trails behind her as she escapes from her stall and charges at me. I have to step sharply to reach the ladder that leads to the loft. I suppose she must think I am after a veal sandwich. Mum's teds close round my trouser leg and I have to wrench free to scramble into the loft. Blimey, it is tough being a peeping tom. People don't realize. We ought to have a flag day.

I shut the trap door and wait for my eyes to become accustomed to the darkness. The light from outside shows me the outline of the shutters and I move forward and ease one of them back a few inches. There is no sign of a light in Miss Tromble's room and the curtains appear to be undrawn. Excellent. A seat in the undress circle and two class performers lined up for an unexpected audition for a large part – well, it will be large by the time I get a gander at the Tromble titties. I settle down beside the opening in the shutters and prepare to wait.

Seconds turn into minutes as is their wont since time immemorial and I am just starting to get anxious when the light in Miss Tromble's room goes on. The woman herself stands framed in the doorway and then closes the door behind her. I concentrate hard: don't close the curtains! Tromble crosses to the window, looks out for several long seconds and then turns round towards the dressing table. Her hands go behind her back and to my great excitement, I see that she is undoing the catches on her blouse – no she isn't, she is taking off a necklace. That's right, girl. Drag it out a bit. She puts the necklace on the dressing table and then her hands go down to her waist. She fiddles with the side of her skirt and down it goes – even faster than sterling. She steps out of it and turns to take a coat hanger from the cupboard. Again she looks towards the window and I hold my breath. It is stupid, really, because there is no chance of her hearing me. Another pause and she hangs up the skirt and returns the hanger to the cupboard.

Now she is standing there in blouse and tights. She looks like an enormous button mushroom. She starts to pull down her tights and sits on the edge of the bed to finish peeling them off. She certainly believes in keeping the best till last. I can't quite see what colour knicks she has on but it looks like white. I will soon know for sure because her hands have gone up to her neck and she is slowly unbuttoning her blouse. She is facing the mirror as she does it but as she slips off the blouse she turns round and – blimey! talk about carnival night at the suet pudding factory. Her top bollocks look ready to run riot at any minute. I don't know where she gets her bras but they would serve as sling shots in a pumpkin-hurling contest.

The blouse is folded up and put in a drawer and Miss Tromble stands in front of her mirror in bra and panties. What a lovely sight. I am practically chanting 'off! off! off!' and I have to confess that wicked percy has found a friend in my naughty fingers. The moment I take him in hand, so to speak, the future does not seem quite so relentlessly unrewarding. A crafty joddrell is a lot better than being left feeling pious and frustrated and – like the man says – you don't have to look your best.

I press my eyeballs nearer to the crack in the shutters and watch, hypnotised, as Betty Tromble bends forward and reaches behind her back. I suppose she does that to stop the bra being ripped from her fingers when she releases the catch. It could burn the flesh right down to the bone. She turns round with the bra between her digits and I suck in breath sharply. By the cringe! What a spectacle. That great, white, flowing mass. I feel like Fred Niagra looking upon his falls for the first time. Wild, untamed, laughing contemptuously in the face of bra manufacturers throughout the world. Imagine your Marquis of Lorne trying to keep its head between that lot. I notice that she has to lift them one at a time. Who says this country is on its knees? Betty Tromble's knockers may be, but the spirit that made a pair like that should have no trouble knocking off a few thousand Hillman Avengers when the need demands. Forty-six inches if she is a day, and British through and through. I am just about to burst into 'There'll always be an England' when she slips off her knicks and exits left.

What a lovely performance. Even better than I had dared hope for. I gaze down and see my knob glistening in the darkness. Its small mouth is twisted up questioningly. Is that all? Very likely, and probably best to indulge in a hand shandy whilst the memory of all that pulsating flesh is still strong in the mind. Still, you never know. It might be worth hanging on a few minutes more. Miss Tromble – or do I know her well enough now to call her Betty? – has probably only popped off to clean her teds and have a pre-kip tinkle. She will be back before you can say unemployment benefit – yes, here she comes, trembling like a stack of blancmanges. She feels under the pillow and produces a long black nightie which she raises above her head and slips over her shoulders with a delicious wriggle – oh! Percy nearly came apart in my hands. I will just see Betty into bed and then give him his head – I would give him my head if I was a monkey. The object of my giggle stick's ill-concealed affection picks up a book – I can't read the title – switches on a bedside lamp and follows her knockers to the door where she turns out the main light. The room is now bathed in a sexy glow and I can see the outline of Betty's body through the veil-like flimsiness of her free-flowing nightie. Oh! I wish I was in there – everywhere. The room, the nightie, Miss Betsy Tromble. I can almost hear the bed creak as she gets into it. She pulls the sheet up underneath her knockers and opens her book. She has to hold it out in front of her or it would be obscured by her manchesters. She must have strong wrists – and talking about strong wrists, time to build up mine with a handy J. Arthur. It is not often that I have recourse to the five-fingered widow but I don't spurn her services when the need arises – sperm but not spurn. I am just about to shake hands with myself when I glance across the courtyard and see Betty putting down her book and glancing towards the door. Can there be someone without apart from me? Miss Tromble gets out of bed and proceeds to answer my question. For some strange reason she stops in front of the mirror to primp up her hair and then she swiftly crosses to the door and opens it. Hardly have her fingers closed round the knob than Gunter materialises beside her as fired through the keyhole from a gas cylinder. Horrible, smarmy berk! What is he brown nosing round there for? Probably going to ask some stupid question about – *blimey*! I don't know whether I say it out loud or not but you could knock me down with a feather. Betty and Ted Gunter are kissing each other! Not so much kissing as trying to eat their way into each other's faces. It is horrible. He must have chloroform breath. Her great knockers are buckling against his chest and he has to lean right forward to get at her cakehole. But getting at it he most certainly is. I would never have thought Ted Gunter could have kissed like that. Now look what he is doing! His horrible germans are molesting Betty's mammaries. I can distinctly see him squeezing her strawberries. What is even more repulsive – she seems to enjoy it. Her head is shaking from side to side and her own hands go up to cover Gunter's on her breasts. The filthy animal plucks open a few buttons and starts gorging his disgusting north and south on her knockers like one of the school's

46

Friesians working over a field of clover. Oh no! It is too horrible to think about, let alone watch. How could she possibly prefer that creep to me. And not an inkling of her obscene passion has she revealed. How mean and sneaky – oh! Before my horrified eyes, Betty starts to make a clumsy assault on the front of Gunter's cavalry twills. With her head tilted back she plucks open the fly and feeds out his cock. What injustice. Why should that idiot get landed with such a length of hose pipe while I have to be content with Mr Average proportions – fifteen and a half centimetres of terribly willing flesh currently doing stark raving nothing? Oh no! It gets worse. Miss Tromble trembles and slowly sinks floorwards, risking getting one of Gunter's shirt buttons up her hooter as she goes. Her face remains buried in his dicky dirt until she is kneeling with her lips inches from his fast-expanding hampton – correction, forget about the inches. Miss Tromble slowly closes her chops round his love lolly and starts revolving her nut like she is trying to exercise her neck muscles. How disgusting! I can hardly bear not to tear my eyes away. Now she has pulled his trousers and pants down to knee level and is milking his balls like she is ringing a peal on a set of bells. Stop! This thing has gone far enough – I am referring, of course, to Gunter's cock. It is expanding faster than Britain's debt to the International Monetary Fund. I have never seen anything like it – even in the magazines Dad used to keep in the hallstand. And quite a lot of those were syrups – renowned for their natural sense of rhythm and jumbo sized tonks.

Not content with what he is getting, Gunter has his hands round the back of Betty's head and is pulling her on to his hampton like he wants to see if he can get it out of one of her earholes. Talk about Deep Throat, this is more like an intravenous rib count. How can she possibly lap this guy up so much? – and I mean lap. Now she looks as if she is trying to swallow one of his balls. I gaze down at once proud percy and he is indeed a sorry sight. A horn all forlorn. Mr Gunter's merry mouthful being taken out for a late night nosh-up is more than he can stand.

Miss Tromble is certainly making a meal of it. I have never known a bird so addicted to guzzling the gonads. Even Gunter must be ready to move on to the next course because he unbuttons his shirt and steps out of his pants and trousers whilst Betty Call-Me-Jaws Tromble continues to stay latched to his chopper. Get your socks off, Gunter! Have you no sense of decency? The man looks like a refugee from a blue film. Pressing his partner back against the floor he kneels astride her treasure chest and slaps her knockers on either side of his hampton. It is like watching someone make bread – enough to feed Birmingham. Whilst I am watching Gunter make a pig of himself I am amazed to see Hollis and Keen come in carrying a tin of beer and a couple of pint mugs. They prop themselves up against the wash basin whilst Gunter leans forward with his hand against the floor and gives Miss Tromble another mouthful of what she likes best after Jimmy Young. Don't tell me that all three are in on this – and even worse – that they invited me along and I turned down the invitation? How could she fancy Hollis, currently pouring beer all over the floor as he tries to get it into a glass. And Keen? Two natural contenders for nana of the year if ever I saw them. It is enough to make you trade in your prick for a skein of wool and a couple of secondhand knitting needles.

Even as the horrible thought permeates my down-the-drain I see Hollis handing down his pint to Gunter for a quick guzzle and lazily stepping out of his round the houses. The Terrible Trio must have been at it since Night One down at the farm to build up such a mood of casual intimacy. By the cringe! It is enough to make you stop watching The Archers. If I had known that Doris and Dan were up to these kind of tricks I would have sprayed my old man with weed killer. How could they, I mean Gunter, Hollis and Keen – not Doris and Dan – have been so much faster on the uptake? It is a bit frightening when you think about it. I thought I was like a greyhound to the nooky. It is clearly not the case. Whilst I am reacting in inhibited fashion to a spot of upper class bridge work others are slamming their nuts into the grinning void – like young Hollis for example. Hardly have his shiny grey worsteds disgraced the carpet than he has said goodbye to his battleship-grey long johns and sunk up to his knees in Axminster. A quick forward shuffle and the bowsprit of his mad mick is steaming between Miss Tromble's swiftly opened thighs – she must have radar to see him through Gunter. As the back of her calves bounce off the new entrant's shoulders, Hollis drives home his dick and holds her scotch eggs apart like he is frightened they might slam shut and carve off his nut. What an amazing turn up. I would have reckoned that the only way he could tell his old man from a carrot was to put it into a vegetable blender and see what colour the juice came out.

Gunter, Hollis and Keen. It sounds like a vaudeville

49

team or a steel works. Hollis hands his pint to Gunter and the rude sod swigs it whilst Tromble continues giving him a blow job. How unrefined! You would never catch me carrying on like that. Any guzzling noises I made always arrived naturally without the help of a keg of Watneys. There seems to be no romance left in the world. I can't understand how Miss Tromble can lend her body to such proceedings. She is obviously much less couth than I took her for. I feel betrayed as I watch her slurping away on the end of Gunter's joint. What can make a woman carry on like that with three such desperate geezers? If I were triplets I could understand it. There is nothing wrong with a cluster fuck if the cluster has a little lustre. This lot make the Three Stooges seem like the ushers at Princess Margaret's wedding.

Keen has now started to take off his clobber but there is no sense of urgency about him. He folds his clothes and places them neatly on the end of the bed, stopping for a pull at his beer between each garment he takes off. I reckon they must have done this before. Probably why Gunter invited me along – to add a bit of variety. But could I have brought myself to perform in such circumstances? – too blooming true I could! Show me an opening and I would not be circling round Betty Tromble's like that daft twit Keen. What are they up to now? Gunter has removed his gleaming dome from Tromble's cakehole and Hollis has withdrawn from her nether regions. Together they draw her to her feet and Hollis slides behind her, cupping her breasts in his hand like a flesh bra. Keen latches his lips on to the erecting nipples and tugs them out gently, drawing his head back until the extended flesh is forced to drop from his lips and the breast falls back on its owner's chest – what a wonderful way to crack walnuts.

Gunter has lain back across the bed and for a moment I think he must have flaked out. Not our boy Gunter. His hampton is still soaring ceilingwards and it is towards this mighty offering that Tromble is steered by Hollis and Keen. I am reminded of Black Magic ceremonies and of Dad and Uncle bringing Aunty Glad home from the plumber's arms – no, I don't mean a pub. That plumber caused Uncle Jack a lot of embarrassment before he ended up with a one-inch nut threaded on his giggle stick. Gunter's plates of meat are on the floor like he has a backwards handstand in mind and Betty runs her fingers up his slippery pole and gives his goolies an affectionate squeeze. Satisfied that the equipment is in working order she positions herself astride his legs and pots his yellow so that two white balls are trembling at the entrance to her centre pocket before you can say Joe Davis – you can see she has played this game before. Secure in the saddle, she leans forward and her champion knockers become a filling between her chest and Gunter's – you can see the white flesh spilling out like cream cheese from a sandwich.

The two love birds kiss memorably and Betty starts to rock backwards and forwards like Lester Piggott coaxing a Derby winner round Tattenham Corner. It is all very affecting and none seems to find it so more than Hollis. Pausing only to shiver his timber with a few strokes of the wrist, he steps between the legs of his two partners in ecstasy and lowers himself to a kneeling position. Surely he can't be intending to? – Oh, he has. Right up to the pollen bags. Betty Tromble buckles for a moment but then returns to rearranging Gunter's features with her kisser in an even greater display of liberated passion. She clearly thrives on this kind of treatment. What a carve-up. I never knew things like this went on south of Dollis Hill.

Now, only Keen has not found a position worthy of his talents and there are just not the openings there were a few minutes ago. The situation is clearly beginning to worry him because he has put down his pint and is circling the frenzied threesome like he hopes that he is going to find something that the others have missed. For a moment he pauses behind Hollis and I fear that I may have to look the other way. For a skinny bloke he has a whopper of a chopper and not, for the first time, I ponder whether this is a reality or my imagination playing tricks – I took my organ to the orgy and nobody asked me to play.

Betty Tromble jerks her mouth off Gunter's cakehole and turns her head sideways to suck in air. I see her twist to look at Hollis and her eye takes in the love feature of the circling Keen – eg he pokes her in the mince pie with it. Introduced at such close quarters, Betty gives the offending article a testing lick and, apparently liking what she tastes, nods her loaf towards the top of the bed. Keen jumps aboard and with legs apart, wriggles down the bed until his spread legs are just above Gunter's head. Betty can and does stretch out her neck and start plating him like she believes she can suck another inch out of his joint. Now she has got three hamptons tucked away and working and it is definitely a bag of sensations that appeals to her. I don't have to get a mike across to her room to know that she is having a good time. The bed is shivering and Keen is reaching down to get his mits under Tromble's Bristols so that he can massage them and gets the winder of his watch entangled in the hair on Gunter's chest – he doesn't mean to, it just happens. Hollis's head goes back and he bares his teeth and it's clear that everyone is about to get their rocks off in one cataclysmic multi-come. What a moment for Betty Tromble. Under fire from three different directions and about to cop a magnum of home perm in the vital apertures. What a way to go. There is a whole lot of shuddering and grabbing as everyone hangs on to their favourite bit and then Keen's head jerks back and bangs against the wall. Gunter's head twists sideways with his eyes closed and his north and south open and Hollis slumps forward with his nut on the small of Betty's back. That friendly soul gives a few hopeful wriggles to see if any life still exists in the interesting parts and then releases Keen's cock like a retriever laying a pygmy shrew at its master's feet. What a change in that once proud organ. From thrusting and throbbing to tiny and tingling. Keen is obviously like me when it comes to the aftermath of a blow job. Very sensitive in the percy department. Hollis pulls out, followed by Gunter and there is a slight argument over ownership of a beer mug. Lucky bastards! All that oggins whilst the Boy Wonder pants in the sidelines. Despite the fact that four up would have put a strain on even Betty Tromble's powers of accommodation I can't help feeling deprived. Percy is now rising between my legs like an Eiffel tower made of flesh and it is hard to tell him that a joddrell is the best he can look forward to. When I think of all the birds lying alone in their beds and thoughtfully running their fingers along the extremities of the velvet void it brings tears to my thighs. If only there was some magic that could bring us together. What a waste of our mutual desires. Suppressing a sigh, I feel in my pocket for my wankerchief and gaze across the yard. My fellow course members – or coarse members as I will now think of them – are clambering into their clothes and looking at their watches. I can imagine Betty Tromble saying that she doesn't want to keep them up too late as they have a busy day tomorrow. She must be well satisfied. I don't think I have ever seen a woman getting it three ways at once. I wonder if I should write to the *Times* – or perhaps *Dalton's Weekly*?

As I start to put percy out of his misery, Gunter, Hollis and Keen take their leave of Betty Tromble and depart with the can of beer. Last of the big spenders. Thank you and good night, gentlemen. Betty looks at herself in the mirror and checks a few bits of flesh that have suffered more than the others. Then she cleans her teeth. Very understandable. I would gargle with harpic, myself. Now, surely, she will go to bed. She returns to the mirror and picks up her hairbrush. Half a dozen strokes and then she crosses to the bed – still with the hairbrush. She lies down and continues with the strokes – but not on her hair. As I watch open-mouthed, the shaft of the hairbrush disappears into her snatch right up to the bristles – both sets – and her left hand stretches out to play with her clit. What a remarkable thing is woman. Three blokes plying her from both ends and still she wants more, or maybe she didn't get what she wanted in the first place – let alone the second place.

My heart leaps only slightly higher than my hampton.

All is not lost. If I nip up to the lady's room she might well be not totally reluctant to grant me an audience. I could say that I was doing some revision and had forgotten the difference between homogenised and pasteurised milk. A spot of sophisticated banter about agricultural subsidies and then down to the pubic press-ups. Stand by romance, here I come

Pausing only to tuck puzzled percy beneath the waistband of my trousers – it is like trying to smuggle a prize cucumber away from the vegetable stand – and I mean stand – I pick my way carefully to the trap door. 'Good evening, Miss Tromble. I wonder if I could have a word with you?' 'Good evening, Miss Tromble. There's something I can't quite get straight.' 'Good evening, Miss Tromble. I've been watching you for the last forty minutes and it occurred to me that we have a mutual problem.' 'Good evening, Miss Tromble. Cop this.' Somewhere between these various approaches must lie the key to Miss Tromble's heart and the bit I am after. I pull up the trap door and – get out of it! Bloody cow! It is waiting exactly where it was when I scrambled into the loft. I stick my foot down and it sinks its teds into my worsted-terylene mixture. I know my trousers are green but this is ridiculous. Doesn't it know one of its own mates when it sees one? Where would it be without me to sell its blooming milk? Dragging round an udder like a barrage balloon. 'Nice Moo-Cow.' Mum always said that I used to like cows when I was a kiddy. It is a pity she didn't tell that to this bleeder – get out of it! I don't want to turn your calf into veal chops! I just want to get out of that door and into Miss Tromble. You know how it is, Daisy. You must have had your moments, otherwise you would not have got lumbered with young Ferdinand there. Step to one side – please! I make a few cajoling noises and lower my foot again – snap! I raise my foot again – fast. All right, Daisy. I hope all your milkmaids have frozen fingers.

Now what am I going to do? No chance of getting through the door without bloodshed. I will have to escape via the window. It is about fifteen feet to the ground but in my present mood I could fly it. I take another glance across the yard and – by the cringe; – Betty Tromble looks as if she is about to go into orbit. She is hopping about like a worm in an ant's nest. Even more committed than when the Three Musketeers were peppering her private parts. Hurry, Lea, there is no time to lose. You don't want to get there and find that she got there already. I know that women are supposed to have about fifty orgasms a bash but at the rate she is going she must be heading for her maiden century.

I find the catch on the dusty, cobweb-covered window and pull. There is a noise like one of my eyeballs coming unstuck after a night on the piss and the window frame scrapes across the floor boards. One of the hinges has come adrift. It is not easy to get out of a window at floor level and in the darkness I have to be careful that I don't snag myself on a nail. It would be a shame to leave my balls behind just when I am going to need them. I feel about the opening and slide my feet out – Space Odyssey 1977. What I am prepared to go through for a stab at the velvet furburger. How I keep copping out on the Honours Lists is a miracle. I slide my feet down the wall and shift my weight to my elbows. If I can just get a grip on this board I will be able to – wheeeeeeeh!

The bloody thing has to be rotten doesn't it? I only have time to push myself away from any nails in the wall before I crash awkwardly on to the cobble stones. Ouch! At first I think I must have broken my ankle. The pain is more than you would wish on the bloke who invented the cinema organ. I feel the swelling and suck in my breath. By the cringe! What a wonderful end to the evening. Crippled and not even a warm glow in my wrists to show for it. I gaze up at Betty Tromble's window and take my first hobbling steps towards the promised gland. As I do so the light goes out.

CHAPTER FIVE

In which Timmy gets to grips with Mrs. Farley who has got a bit behind – she has not been paying her bills either.

'How's the ankle?' says Mr Claygate.

'Much better, thanks,' I say.

'I'm sorry you missed Mr Glossop's farewell party. It was very affecting. Thirty years is a long time.'

'Very,' I say.

'I put in thirty pence on your behalf – for the collection, I mean. I'll deduct it from your next wages.'

'Thanks a lot,' I say. 'What did I give him?'

Claygate looks at me sharply and strokes his moustache. '*We* gave him a clock. He expressed a preference.' Claygate sighs. 'With him passes an era. Meadowfresh will never be the same again.' I nod brightly. 'Still, I'm not saying that that's a bad thing. This firm is ripe for a shake-up. Time doesn't stand still, you know.' I look serious. 'The business is a lot more competitive nowadays. People aren't too choosy about how they get new customers. The weakest go to the wall. Get me?'

My eyes narrow into slits. When Claygate talks to me like a hired gun my mind goes back to the doctor who was called to the Meadowfresh Residential Course when I did my ankle. He went into Betty Tromble's room to get some cold water for a compress and didn't come out for two hours. National Health Service? It would be better if they issued them with humane killers the moment they left medical school.

'Are you listening to me, Lea?'

'Oh yes, Mr Claygate. You were telling me about Mr Glossop's clock.'

'I'd moved on from that,' says Claygate irritably. 'I was on to my plans for expansion. It was more difficult when Glossop was here. He was – how shall I put it?'

'A stupid old twit?' I say helpfully.

Claygate winces. 'Reactionary was the word I was looking for. Finding it difficult to move with the times. My plans need young blood.'

'Oh yes,' I say. The last time I heard about plans like that it was in *The News of The World – Vampire Brownies of New Malden* was, I believe, the name of the article.

'I want malleable young men,' says Claygate.

'They're from Africa, aren't they?' I say. 'They'll certainly show up well against the milk.'

'Malleable meaning mouldable,' grits Claygate. 'Flexible. Capable of facing up to every challenge as it arises – and believe me, Lea, there are going to be changes. I'm going to dynamise this place, do you understand me?'

'You mean, blow it up and claim the insurance?' I say. 'Yes, I like the sound of that. Where do you want me to put the—'

'No!' Claygate closes his eyes and I see the whites of his knuckles. 'I am going to make it a repository of modern marketing techniques. I am going to instigate a whole new approach to selling dairy products – notice, I don't just say milk. I intend to widen our range.'

And drive out those pesky sheep farmers once and for

all, I muse to myself. When he talks like that you feel you are listening to Burl Ives geeing up the lads for a spot of Western aggro. Not that Claygate is all that overwhelming a personality. I know that he followed the BBC Management Today course except when the wife's mother came to dinner and when he had to get a grip on the garden, but as a manager he seems to live more in hope than experience.

'We've got to get more customers,' he continues. 'It's as simple as that. The cows are performing their side of the bargain. Now it's up to us.'

'More canvassing,' I say.

Claygate nods. 'It's not just a question of doing it – it's how you do it. Frankly, Lea, this is a ticklish question.' He looks about him and lowers his voice. 'I don't know if you've ever thought about it but ninety-five per cent of our customers are women.'

'Now you mention it – ' I say, a note of wonder entering my voice.

'Sex appeal, Lea.' Claygate blushes. 'It comes in the reckoning, you know. If you can project yourself you could win a new customer.' I pretend to consider this earth shattering proposition. Claygate leans forward confidentially. 'I couldn't have had this conversation with Glossop. He wouldn't have known what I was talking about.'

'No,' I say.

'I hope I'm not shocking you,' says Claygate. 'I'm not asking you – or any of the other lads – to get involved in any hanky panky. Just flaunt yourselves a little bit. Let the customer know that she's a woman and that you appreciate the fact.'

'Blimey,' I say.

'Comes as a bit of a surprise to you, I expect,' says Claygate. 'You look like a lad that has led a sheltered life.'

'Well—' I begin.

'Nothing to be ashamed of in that. I'm not advocating licence. It's just that we've got to keep up with the dodges the others are using. That's the thinking behind the new uniforms.'

'I didn't know we had uniforms,' I say.

'Only a cap,' says Claygate. 'Made you look a bit like a bus conductor. I've scrapped that. Now it's a one piece white tunic with the Meadowfresh crest on the breast pocket and your name embroidered in italic lettering across the back: "Timmy". It's more friendly than Timothy, isn't it? There's also a white cap with a long peak.'

'Blimey,' I say. 'All I need is a baseball bat. Where did you get all these ideas from?'

'Most of them are things I've been thinking about for some time,' says Claygate breezily. 'The others were sparked off by discussions with the new man I took on while you were recuperating. Very forward looking, he is.'

A faint feeling of unease flickers through my subconscious. 'New man?' I say.

'If we're going to expand, we've got to have more salesmen – or vendors. I think "vendor" sounds better, don't you? Got a ring of class about it. Would you rather be a vendor or a salesman?'

'A salesman,' I say. 'A vendor would make me feel like I had a coffee dispenser where my belly button ought to be. Who is this bloke?'

'Nugget,' says Claygate. 'No, wait a minute – Nogget.

Sidney Garth Noggett. Interesting man. Very experienced. Done a lot of things. Couldn't wait to get on the job.'

'That's Sid, all right,' I say.

'You know him?' says Claygate.

'He's my brother-in-law,' I say. 'Married my sister Rosie.'

'He didn't mention that,' says Claygate.

'I expect he wanted to give me a surprise,' I say. 'Where is he now?'

'He's out with one of the lads,' says Claygate cheerfully. 'I told him that despite his superior qualifications he still had to start at the bottom – just like you did.'

'Very democratic,' I say.

'It has to be,' says Claygate seriously. 'Of course, when he comes back from his course I'll probably make him up.'

'Make him up?' I say. 'You mean promote him?'

'I don't mean send him out to buy an eyebrow pencil from Boots,' says Claygate. 'Oh yes, I think a management structure is what this company needs. It's going to be expensive at first but I'm prepared to mortgage the present in order to purchase the future.'

'Why do you think Sid has had so many jobs?' I say, trying to keep calm.

'He told me that,' says Claygate, clearing his throat. 'His mother. The incurable disease – '

'It's not incurable,' I say. 'A couple of penicillin shots and—'

'He kept having to go back and nurse her. I think when he was ahead in the single-handed trans-Atlantic yacht race, that must have been the worst time. Getting the wireless message when he was becalmed and having to swim back past the other contestants. How many days was it before the Captain of the *QE2* heard him hammering on the hull? Two? Three?'

'At least,' I say, deciding that I might as well throw in the sponge while I still have the strength. 'Ah well, Mr Claygate. What do you want me to do? Take over Mr Glossop's round?'

'I've rejigged all the areas,' says Claygate. 'There was too much complacency creeping in. Now everything is up for grabs. The customers are going to see some new faces and you're going to see some new customers. Try on your new uniform, take your float off charge and go out and conquer Balham!'

'Off to a Meadowfresh start,' I say.

Claygate wags his finger at me admiringly. 'Excellent!' he says. 'We could use that as a slogan.'

He is still happily repeating the phrase as I glide out of the front gates on my float. George Claygate is a nice bloke but he shows the same judgement of character as a bird picking Hitler's photograph on a computer dating form. Fancy getting lumbered with Sid again. I feel dead narked, especially after all the cobblers he was spouting about not touching the noble profession of milkman with my old man wrapped in pipe lagging. Typical that having said that he should give Claygate a complete grease job. What a slimy bugger he is.

I am still fretting as I pull up outside One Phillibeach Gardens, my first port of call. That address has a red cross beside it in my little book but not because a bird in nurse's uniform takes your temperature when you ring the front door bell. Mrs Farley is apparently four weeks behind with her milk bill. Meadowfresh's terms are strictly pay-up every seven days, but a blind eye is turned to two weeks and nobody gets their knickers in too much of a twist if three weeks go by without an injection of geldt. It is only after twenty-one days that blokes like me are supposed to start winkling out the ackers and if necessary recommend legal action. Nobody likes doing that because it costs money and loses a customer.

'Ah, good morning, madam.' The bird in front of me is all fluffy and dithery and dressing while I look at her. She fiddles with the buttons of her blouse – just fiddles, doesn't do any of them up – and occasionally pats her hair and the back of her arse like she wonders if she put a skirt over it. 'Mrs Farley?'

'That's right. What can I do for you?' She shoves her knockers forward a couple of inches and smiles nervously.

'I'm your new milkman,' I say.

She cranes her head over my shoulder and takes a gander at the float. Her face clouds over. 'Oh,' she says. 'I've got a bit behind, haven't I?'

'You've got a bit in front, as well,' I say, ever prepared to soften the blow with a spot of humour.

Mrs Farley blushes and quickly does up a couple of buttons. She need not have bothered. 'I don't know if I can do it,' she says. 'It's been a difficult week. You'd better come in. Would you like a cup of tea while I see what I've got?'

'That's very kind of you,' I say. 'They're getting a bit worried down at the depot,' I add that so she does not think that I am going to be an easy touch: eg one cup of Rosie Lea and ta, ta till next week.

The net curtains around us are waving like a semaphore contest and Mrs Farley notices my glance. 'They've got dirty minds,' she says, closing the door firmly. 'Any woman living on her own has to put up with it. They'd believe you were having an affair with every man who came to the door. How do you like it?'

'I beg your pardon?' I say.

'Your tea?'

'Oh, any way it comes. Ta.'

We are in the kitchen now and Mrs Farley moves the brand new Sony cassette-playing transistor from the table to a new-looking fridge which still has a price ticket on it. 'A present,' she says indicating the transistor. 'My mum's been very good to me in my time of need. Now, how much do I owe?'

'Well,' I say. 'Four weeks at-er-um-yes, and the-yes. That's eight pounds, sixty-three pence.'

Mrs Farley pauses with her teapot above my cup. 'Eight pounds sixty-three pence! That can't be right. I've never drunk that much milk.'

'You had the juice,' I remind her.

'What Jews?' Mrs Farley turns scarlet. 'What have you heard? It's the neighbours, isn't it? Just because the man who collects for the loan club is a bit dark-skinned – and why shouldn't he bring his brother to look at the vacuum cleaner. Were they supposed to mend it in the garden? Really, I've had about enough of their dirty, prying—'

'Orange juice!' I shout. 'And don't forget the two dozen eggs and the butter.'

Mrs Farley stops shaking long enough to direct some of the tea into my cup. 'Oh yes,' she says. 'Silly of me.

That's what happens to you, living around here. You become confused. I'll have to move.'

'I hope you can settle up with us before you go,' I say.

Mrs Farley looks hurt. 'That's not very nice,' she says. 'I invite you in for a cup of tea and you accuse me of being a thief.'

'Oh no,' I say. 'I didn't mean anything like that. You misunderstood me.'

Mrs Farley sits down and rests her head in her hands. 'It's no good,' she says. 'I can't go on.' Then she starts to cry.

Oh dear. I am always bleeding hopelesss when women start crying. 'Look,' I say, 'don't cry. That's not going to help. How much have you got?'

Mrs Farley doesn't say anything but continues to sob. I drink my cha and see her watching me through a gap in her fingers. One large reproachful eye. 'Being called a thief. That's the last straw.'

'I didn't call you a thief,' I say.

'You did. I heard you. Is that how they teach you to behave at the depot? Mr Turberville would never have carried on like that.' (Turberville was the bloke before me. Big, soft fellow with a limp.) 'I think I'll report you to the manager. I've had enough persecution.' She starts to sob again.

'Have a cup of tea,' I say. 'You'll feel better. It's nothing to get worked up about. Really it isn't.' I nearly say I'll come back next week but I just stop myself. I must see this thing through if I can. I get up and grab the teapot. It is nearly empty. I put it down and give Mrs Farley what is supposed to be a reassuring pat on the shoulder.

'Why did you touch me?' she says, staring up into my face.

'No reason,' I say. 'I just didn't want you to worry, that's all.'

Mrs Farley rises to her feet and advances on me. She has stopped crying very quickly. 'You're like the rest of them, aren't you?' she says. 'Trying to make something out of my predicament.'

'I don't know what you mean,' I say. 'I'm here purely on behalf of Meadowfresh.'

'Purely?' she says. 'Don't make me laugh. You know I can't pay so you're going to take advantage. I suppose you'd like to have me on the kitchen table.'

'Mrs Farley—' I begin, but she is already moving the teapot.

'You don't have to say anything,' she says. 'I've heard it all before. If I give in to your demands, you'll give me a week's extension?'

I don't know about a week's extension but she has already won herself a couple of inches. Percy is like a groin greyhound when it comes to homing in on a potential bout of in and out.

'Please, Mrs Farley,' I splutter. 'You have the wrong end of the stick. I had no intention of trying to compromise you. I just want the money – and please put your knickers on again.'

'I hope someone will find it in their hearts to forgive you for this,' says Mrs Farley hopping up on to the edge of the table and throwing her panties over her shoulder so that they land on the new toaster – no doubt another present from mum. 'Make it short.'

Whatever she is talking about, it isn't percy. My action

68

man kit is letting Meadowfresh down in a big way. Oh dear, it is all so difficult. Mr Claygate was talking about getting closer to the customers but I reckon that he might think inside was a bit too close. Especially in these circumstances.

'What are you waiting for? Are you trying to humiliate me?' Mrs Farley feels my nether cosh and plucks open the buttons that run down the front of my new uniform. 'Could have been designed for the job,' she husks. 'Ooh. Here we are. You dirty brute, you should be ashamed of yourself.'

'Mrs Farley – ' I begin. But it is too late. She has introduced my old man to her snatch faster than a new recruit to a Tupperware circle and lain back with her head on a packet of Ryvita. How different from the home life of our dear Queen. I would like to talk to her – I mean, Mrs Farley, of course – but the lady has closed her eyes and is jerking her head from side to side and heaving her not inconsiderable bosom. I lean forward to move the Ryvita – waste not, want not – but Mrs Farley pushes me back firmly.

'Don't leave me!' she commands. 'Ooh! Could you see your way to an extra pint?'

For a moment, I wonder what she is talking about. I was thinking in terms of a couple of fluid ounces at the most. Then it dawns on me. 'Listen,' I say. 'This has gone far enough.'

'No, it hasn't!' Her legs scissor round my back and her clit makes a cleft in the bit where my cock joins my pelvis for the summer holidays. I wish I could say that I was impervious to all this but since I am not quite sure what it means, I won't. Suffice to say that Mrs Farley's charms are getting through to me. In for a penny, in for a pounding, as they say. The lady's berkeley is one with more drawing power than Manchester United and it is difficult to remain totally in control of your scruples when your mad mick is enjoying a sensation like being choked in velvet. I don't feel I can withdraw without turning the bird inside out.

'OOOOAAAARRRRRWWWWWWGGGGG ! ! ! ! !' Blimey! That was the Chivers Olde Englishe Marmalade. A direct hit from the clenched fist riccocheting the contents of the saucer half way round the table.

'WOWF!' A mighty kung fu blow crunches through a pile of Weetabix. Mrs Farley clearly does not care when she is in the mood. Now her fingers have got caught in the toast rack. How genteel. She prises them free and starts sucking the wounded digits. Very sexy. I brace my thighs against the edge of the table and start dishing out the love thrusts. Firm but controlled. My hands patrol Mrs Farley's breasts and her own clamp on top of them. They are sticky. Not surprising really after the marmalade.

'That's it!' she says. 'Go on, go on!'

I can't help feeling a bit choked when they talk like that. I have been going on all the time. It is just that she has suddenly caught up with what I am doing. Women! It is always the wrong thing at the right time, or the right thing at the wrong time, or the wrong thing at the wrong time, or the right thing at the right time – only they changed their minds the moment you start doing it. They are so bloody difficult. For two pins and a bacon slicer down the front of my Y-fronts I would jack the whole thing in and start collecting train numbers – it wouldn't take long to get all of them the way things are going at the moment.

'Don't stop!' I was not stopping. I was just slowing down to make sure that my balls didn't drop into the cutlery drawer. She only has to start tidying up in mid-chava and her old man could cop a nasty surprise the next time he looked for a bottle opener – 'Have you taken up golf, Marcia?' Stranger things have happened. I remember a bird who kept patting the pillows all the time I was giving her one. She had spent twenty minutes folding the counterpane, too. Hardly carried away in a tidal wave of passion.

The kitchen table is now looking like a battle ground. The Grapenuts have spilled into the marmalade and a fine dust of Weetabix covers the scene. It is not the only one around. As I look down to the point where my Marquis of Lorne is pursuing its leisurely passage into Mrs Farley's fun box I observe a cloud of black powder dancing in the air. How exotic. I have known women to powder their snatches but never with black talcum. What a rich harvest of experience the lady is turning out to be. Turned on by the sight, I take a firm grip of her thighs and start wacking in the love thrusts. It is satisfying enough but not, I soon discover, as effective as me standing still and pulling her on to me like a wheelbarrow. The tablecloth ruckles and stretches like the side of a concertina and a familiar sensation starts to quiver through my dick. Could be that the local sperm bank is going to be denied another deposit – 'Ooooooh!' Very nice, even if the butter does fall on the cat – how did that get in here? It looks at me disapprovingly and then licks its paw and sweeps it behind its ear. That means rain, doesn't it?

71

Not to worry. I don't really care at the moment. Hot currents of velvety syrup are fanning out through my loins and Mrs Farley is the only thing left on the table.

'Wheeeeeeh!' The cat blinks and Mrs Farley claps her hand round my bum and hangs on for dear life. A couple of thrusts and my dick is gripped with the fervour of an American Presidential candidate's handshake. A mighty, muscular mechanism gets to work and the fruit of my loins is harvested so fast that you can almost hear a noise like a suction cleaner in full slurp. There would be no question of coypu interrupted with this lady – not unless you were prepared to leave your dick behind.

'Have you finished?' The question is purely academic as they say. Mrs Farley has her feet on the floor before I have tucked my hampton away. 'So,' she says. 'You got what you wanted. I'll make sure I've got the money next week so I'm spared a similar ordeal.'

'Er – yes, the money,' I say. 'I was wondering – ' But it is no good. She is already walking towards the door and I can't bring myself to make an issue of it. She has got round me – huh, you can say that again. I put the remains of the Grapenuts back on the table and follow her to the door. 'Well – er, next week then,' I hear myself say. 'I'm sorry to push it but we're having a bit of a drive on – ' I break off when I find that I am talking to the door which has been closed in my face. I turn away and twenty net curtains drop like guillotines. I glance down and my shirt is poking out of my fly. Charming. I re-arrange it and look up the street. Interesting. That solves the mystery of the black talcum. Three houses away, the coalman is coming out of the front gate.

CHAPTER SIX

In which Timmy becomes involved with Sue Dangerfield
of the Milk Marketing Board and a dissatisfied customer.

'Reminds me of the bloke who wanted to buy his missus
a talking parrot,' says Sid.

'Why did he want to do that?' I ask.

'Because he was away a lot and he thought she'd like
someone to talk to,' says Sid. 'Stop interrupting and get
the beer in. Now, where was I? – oh yes. He goes round
to the pet shop and he says 'How are you off for talking
parrots?' And the geezer says: 'Fantastic. You couldn't
have come at a better time. I've got this fantastic little
number. Wonderful talker. Only problem is – it doesn't
have any legs.' So the bloke says: 'Well, how does he stay
on his perch?' And the geezer says: 'Easy, he wraps his
old man round it.' So the bloke thinks for a bit and he
has a chat with the parrot – who *is* a lovely talker – and
in the end he decides to have him. He takes the bird home
and his old lady is dead chuffed. She loves the bloody
parrot. So the bloke is highly satisfied and goes off and
leaves his wife with the parrot. Two weeks later, he
comes back and his wife isn't in. Only the parrot is there.
So he says: 'Afternoon. Everything going all right?' And
the parrot says: 'Very nicely, thank you. Only one thing
– I'm a bit worried about the milkman.' So the bloke
pricks up his ears and says: 'What do you mean?' And
the parrot says: 'Well, couple of days after you left, the
milkman came round and your wife asked him in for a

73

cup of tea.' 'Oh yes?' says the bloke.' 'Yes,' says the parrot. 'And he's no sooner through the door than your missus has got his old man out.' 'That's terrible,' says the bloke. 'I thought so too.' says the parrot. 'But there was worse to come.' 'What happened?' says the bloke who is now getting highly agitated. 'She let him take her knicks off and then she got up on the kitchen table.' By now the bloke is sweating blood. 'What happened?' he shouts. 'Come on, you've got to tell me!' And he grabs the parrot by the neck and starts shaking it. 'The milkman took his trousers off and got between your wife's legs,' gasps the parrot. 'And then what?' sobs the bloke. 'I don't know,' says the parrot. 'I got a hard on and fell off my perch.'

Sid falls about and I try to catch the barman's eye. Blokes who rolled up at the bar yonks after me are getting served, but Lea? – not a sausage. It never seems to work like that on films. The hero only has to raise an eyebrow and eight waiters are knocking people down to get to him.

'Great story, isn't it?' says Sid. 'You can just see the old parrot keeling off its perch, can't you?'

'Sid,' I say. 'What made you change your mind about becoming a milkman?'

'You're not still on about that, are you?' say Sid. 'Anyone can change their mind, you know. It was my conversation with your Mr Claygate that did it. Nice fellow. He's got a lot of interesting ideas. I was at one with him in many areas. What's the crumpet situation like on this course?'

'Terrible,' I say. 'There's this bird with big knockers but she's just not interested. I heard her telling someone that sex turns her right off. I think she's got something wrong with her, too.'

'Probably cyclepneumatic,' says Sid. 'Don't worry, I'll sort her out in no time. The ones who say they don't like it are always a pushover. They're frightened, that's all. What they need is a bloke who's prepared to trample over their scruples. They want to be mastered. They want somebody to do the thinking for them. They want to be swept off their feet. For instance: when you open a packet of crisps, you keep the salt to yourself. If they want any they have to come to *you*.'

'It's a whole new world,' I say.

'Course it is,' says Sid. 'Hey, Gunga Din. You ever thought of serving beer in this place? It's not a bleeding temple, you know.' The Indian bloke behind the bar does not take kindly to this remark and I judge it wise to take my leave when Sid starts complaining to the manager that the bitter tastes of curry powder. I don't have a lot of time to waste anyhow because the sooner I finish my round and plug in my float on the charger, the sooner I can piss off for the day. You have to get up early but you can leave yourself a lot of spare time if you want to. Some blokes do two jobs but I am not that crazy about making money. Sid is keeping his reasons for joining Meadowfresh pretty dark but I reckon it must be more than taking a shine to Claygate's mug. He has got some crafty little scheme up his sleeve.

'Yoo hoo! Timothy Lea?' I look up and there is a very nice little number wearing a blue suit with an MMB badge on the lapel. She is leaning out of the window of a Morris 1100.

'In the flesh,' I say. 'Every glorious, glistening inch of me.'

'Don't be a chump,' she says. 'I'm from the Milk Marketing Board. Sue Dangerfield spending a day with you chaps trying to gee up sales. Don't expect you knew anything about it. Absolutely lousy communications.'

'Mr Claygate didn't say anything,' I say. 'At least, I don't think he did.'

'It doesn't matter,' says the bird. 'We'll be able to get on with it, won't we?'

'No trouble,' I say. 'What exactly did you have in mind?'

'Well, it's pretty boring, most of it. A few recipe leaflets about things to do with that extra pinta. Then there's a little competition they can enter for if they buy something. You ought to know all about this. There were tons of forms.'

'Maybe they arrived when I was on my course,' I say. 'Er – how are we travelling?'

'I'll go with you. We can pick the car up later if that's all right with you. I must say, it does make a change to be with a young chap. Some of the ones I've been with in the last few days have been real old fogies. No zip at all. Frankly, I've been rather disappointed. I mean, back at HQ the gels look forward to going up the sharp end.'

'How very unusual,' I say.

'In the field,' she says. 'It's all very well making graphs about milk yields and the effect of rain on calf production but you yearn to get out where the action is. I mean, the milkman is a key figure in our childhood, isn't he?'

'I suppose he is,' I say. 'To tell you the truth I hadn't

76

thought about it a lot.' I stop the float and grab hold of a few tubes.

'The familiar jangle of the crates. The cheerful, toothy grin. I think the milkman was more familiar than my father when I was a little girl.'

'It's quite possible,' I say, shoving open the garden gate with my bum. Sue pads up the path behind me.

'Mummy can remember when he had a horse.'

'Your old man? What was he, a cowboy?'

'Don't be silly. I'm talking about the milkman.'

I put the pintas in the shade and pick up the empties. Nicely rinsed out. Just the way I hope to find them. 'Do you want to do a bit of chat?'

Sue shakes her head. 'I don't stop at every house. If I did I'd never be finished.' She looks at me searchingly. 'What made you decide to be a milkman?'

'Dunno,' I say. 'It's a job, isn't it? Open air, you're on your own. I prefer that.'

'It's funny,' she says. 'The stories you hear.' She is looking at me out of the corner of her eye, watching my reaction.

'Stories?' I shove the empties into the crate.

'About milkmen. Like window cleaners.'

'I used to be a window cleaner too,' I say.

Sue's eyes widen. 'Did—er anything happen?' I look at her. 'I mean, did anybody proposition you?'

'You mean, make a pass at me?'

'That kind of thing.'

'That would be telling, wouldn't it?' I help myself to some more milk and start up another garden path. Sue's interest bodes well but I sense that it will pay to play her along a bit.

77

'You never hear anything about postmen. That's funny, isn't it?'

'It's not a very glamorous uniform. And delivering bills and all that. It doesn't exactly put you in the mood, does it? Still, I believe the blokes who did the North Sea Gas conversions had a few laughs.'

'The opportunity to get inside the house must make a difference.'

'You've really thought about it, haven't you?'

'I'm fascinated by the idea of women making love to a perfect stranger.'

'He's not a stranger. If you roll up at a bird's house every day, you're part of the scenery.' I bend down and pick up the piece of paper stuck in the empty milk bottle. It reads 'Door not locked. Please pop milk in fridge. Thank you, Ellen Grant.' 'See what I mean?' I say, handing Sue the note. 'She's quite happy for me to poke around inside her house.' I didn't mean anything by my choice of words but from the way Sue looks at me I can see that she may have got the wrong impression.

'I'll pop in, just in case she's lurking,' she says. 'What kind of things do they say?'

'You mean, if they fancy you? Oh, they might suggest a cup of tea.' I open the front door and Sue follows me inside clutching her leaflets. 'It's more a question of their general behaviour though.'

'What do you mean?'

'Well, if they seem really pleased to see you and give you lots of chat. Drop little hints about how they bet you get involved in some funny situations.'

'Like me, in fact?' says Sue.

'That's right,' I say coolly. 'Then there's the way they

78

dress. If they've made a special effort and you can niff a pong of perfume that's always favourite. Chanel Number Five often leads to Channel Number One.'

'How coarse.' Sue gives a ladylike shiver.

'Well you did ask. Open the door, will you?'

Sue does what I ask and looks round the small kitchen. 'And this is where you sit with your cup of tea, is it? Swopping small talk and sizing up the situation.'

'That's right,' I say. 'But I can't hang about because the battery on the float might run down and I'd have to push it back to the depot. Do you fancy a bit?' I have got the door of the fridge open and she peers over my shoulder at a bowl of dripping.

'That?'

'A bit of the other. What you're so interested in.'

'Don't be ridiculous!'

'You've talked about nothing else. I'd have thought you were doing a survey on the sex life of a milkman.'

'My interest is purely academic. I didn't mean to give you any ideas.'

'I started getting ideas the first moment I saw you.'

'Don't be silly.'

'I'm not being silly. You're a knockout looking bird. Fantastic eyes.' What is encouraging about this conversation is that the lady from the Milk Marketing Board is showing no sign of moving towards the door.

'This is stupid. We've only just met. I think I'll leave a leaflet. After all, she did invite us in.'

'Let's make the most of it. Hop upstairs for a few minutes. Nobody's going to be any the wiser.'

'You're mad. Supposing she came back?'

'She won't come back. That's why she left the note.

Oh, Sue – ' I grab her to me and dive on to her small, pink mouth. 'You really are so beautiful.' Don't ever underestimate the importance of telling a bird she is beautiful. They can never hear it enough. You could go round the world on 'You are beautiful' in forty-two languages.

Sue breaks away from me and looks searchingly into my eyes. I try and adopt an expression which combines passionate sincerity with sincere passion. This is a vital moment. Sue sighs a sigh that could mean anything. Eventually, she speaks, 'I'll have to go to the bathroom.'

When she comes out, I have located the back bedroom and turned down the bedspread. I am very thoughtful like that. She has still got her suit on and is clearly going through the second thoughts stage so beloved of women. 'We shouldn't be doing this,' she says.

I take her hand. It is cold and presumably freshly washed. The chill touch has the opposite effect to cooling me down. 'Come on,' I say. I give her my look of scarce-concealed animal desire and draw her after me towards the bedroom.

'Do you do this a lot?' she says. 'Ooh. I don't like this wallpaper.'

'Try looking at the ceiling,' I say, pushing her gently backward on to the bed.

'I couldn't sleep with those curtains,' she says, her hands going automatically to her shoulders.

'You won't have to.' I help her off with her jacket and sit down on the bed so that I can kiss her while I undo the buttons down the front of her blouse. 'That's a very pretty bra. It deserves you.'

'It's French,' she says. 'They have some lovely things.'

'So do you,' I murmur, gently pinching one of her

nipples through the material. 'You've got a marvellous figure.'

I unbutton her blouse and then slip my hands round the small of her back so that I can unhook her bra. I sense that she is a bit shy and that it would be a bad move to pull everything off before she is warmed up. I also prefer birds when they are half-undressed. It is more sexy somehow. 'You didn't answer my question,' she says.

'Which one?' I take her lower lip between my teeth and bite it ever so gently.

'About whether you do this often – oooh!' I have slipped my hand under her hanging bra and started drawing circles round her raspberries.

'Do you like that?'

'Uhm,' She leans forward and suddenly starts licking my ear. 'I suppose that answers my question?'

I don't say anything but lower my head between her breasts and start following the pattern of my fingers with my tongue. Her bristols hang beautifully following the curve of a crescent moon lying on its back. I nuzzle the teats with my nose and then rasp my tongue along their tips before taking them, one by one, into my mouth.

Sue shivers and digs her fingers into my back. 'Yum!' she says. 'Now the other one, please.' Her hands move round to the front of my shirt and she unbuttons it swiftly. 'You're making me want you,' she says.

'That's the idea.' I lift my head from her breasts and she kisses me hard on the mouth, pushing her hand clumsily between my legs.

'It's very bad to wear tight jeans.'

'I'd better take them off.' We rise in unison and I strip off my shirt and unbuckle my belt. I pull down the zip and percy tumbles out like a pack of hounds from the back of a van.

Sue looks down in the middle of taking off her skirt and shakes her head. 'I don't know how there's room for him in there,' she says.

'He folds flat for travelling,' I say. I step out of my shoes and sit down on the bed so that I can feed off my jeans, pants and socks in what is meant to be one flowing movement. It doesn't work out quite like that because I have to grit my teeth to force my jeans over my heels. Sue slips off her bra and blouse and is now down to her panties. She starts to take them off and then pulls them up again.

'You can take them off,' she says.

It is funny how birds like you to take their knickers off. Maybe it has something to do with a subconscious desire to be violated. Or maybe if you take them off they don't feel that they are giving themselves too easily – or they feel that they are not really giving themselves at all, the whole thing is being done by you. Or maybe they just like having their knickers taken off. Either way, I am always happy to oblige. Especially with a chick like Sue. The suit does not do her justice. She is a right little bundle of curves without it. She sits down on the bed and sticks out a finger to pat my mad mick.

'He looks so red and angry,' she says. 'You really shouldn't coop him up like that.'

'Maybe I should wear him sticking out all the time,' I say. 'I wouldn't get very far, would I?'

'You would with some people,' she says. And, blow me up and down, before you can say 'light the blue touch paper and retire immediately' she has lowered her beautiful little head into my lap and slapped her rose lips round my delighted dongler. What a nice girl. The refined ones are often the best. I lie back across the bed and cop the lovely view of her nut bobbing up and down while her hair flops down like a modesty curtain. What a performer. She could see off a tray of ice cubes in thirty seconds without drawing breath. Thank goodness I got that book out of Battersea Public Library which taught me all about control. How the great lovers think about their Y-fronts being full of walnut shells so that they don't come their load. The art of stopping yourself enjoying what you are enjoying so that you can go on enjoying it for longer. Blooming stupid, really. If I followed by natural inclination I would treat Sue to a mad mick milkshake and get my head down for a nice little kip – and talking of getting my head down. Yes, I had better do more for my keep than help Susan develop bow lips. I slide my hand round her back bumpers and slip my fingers inside her panties. The flesh is firm and stretched as she bends forwards and I work into the cleft and then follow it round till I am tickling her dilly pot. It is moist as an oyster.

'Come on,' I pull her up on to my mouth and push her panties down while we kiss. I am alternately sucking her tongue and pushing my own deep into her cakehole to give her a taste of what she can look forward to. Her panties are down around her thighs, a tight band of blue, and I press the palm of my hand against her pelvic bone and dabble my fingers in the trench that runs beneath it. She begins to moan and I press harder and lay her whole body back against the bed. She looks up at me with her lips trembling and I slide off her panties and lean forward so that I can part her lower lips and run my tongue down the already slippery channel. Not entirely by accident, my hampton is parked outside her north and south and gratitude is one of the sensations I experience when she once again uses him to part her lips. The classic sixty-nine – or soixante-neuf as they call it in Birmingham. Down goes my head and I press firmly into snatchville trying to take as much of that article into my mouth as I can. Sue's thighs are clamped on either side of head and – ouch! A stinging slap on the bum makes me wonder if she is kinky for violence. I look up and – oh dear. There is a middle-aged lady I have never seen before and she is bristling, literally bristling. Summing the situation up in a glance, I do what comes naturally – panic.

'Oh, sorry. Didn't hear you coming – ha, ha, er – yes. I'm your new milkman. This young lady is from the Milk Marketing Board. Would you like a recipe leaflet? – take two, take some for your friends. Very good for you, milk. Lots of energy and a rich, creamy complexion. How about a competition? I can enter you if you like—' the woman's expression changes from alarm to horror ' – in the competition, of course, ha, ha.'

If only my cock would stop bouncing up and down while I am talking. 'How dare you!'

'I know,' I say. 'I'm very sorry. We got carried away. I put the cat in the fridge – I mean, the milk in the fridge. Are you sure you won't go in for the competition? Miss Dangerfield, could you spare a moment to run through the details?'

Sue is dressing so fast that you would think the house

was on fire. 'It's very simple,' she says, shoving her blouse into her skirt and trying to smile. 'It's all about the countryside.'

The woman snorts. 'With a special accent on the farm-yard, I suppose?'

'Oh yes,' I say. 'Very jovial. I'm glad you can accept our little escapade in the light-hearted manner in which it was—'

'Silence, you dolt!' interrupts the woman. 'Your tongue has done enough damage for one afternoon.'

'Er – yes,' I say. 'Well, we'd better get on the job again – ha, ha.'

The woman winces and looks at Sue in a not unkindly fashion. 'You're worthy of better things, my dear,' she says. 'Let this horrible experience be a lesson to you. Do not let your standards tumble into the gutter. Contact with this kind of man can only soil you.'

'Even if I give Green Shield stamps?' I say.

The woman grits her teeth. 'They will know what to do with you at the Depot.'

'Please,' I say. 'Don't report me. I'll do anything.'

The woman's face softens a fraction. 'Anything?'

'Well, almost anything,' I say. 'I couldn't teach Anthony Wedgwood Benn to french kiss.'

'That will not be necessary.'

'Thank you,' I say. 'I – ' my voice dies away as I see that the woman is glancing at me in a very funny way. A thoughtful expression is occupying those parts of her mug not currently covered by an overabundance of facial hair. She looks down towards my feet and then up again. Surely she can't be – ? I quickly pull my underpants over my still-rampant cock – too quickly as it turns out –

85

and start to back towards the door, picking up clothes along the way.

'Miss Dangerfield,' I say. 'We'd better—'

'No!' Oh no. The woman clearly has plans for my firm young flesh which are too horrible even for a new television sit-com series. The sight of proud percy soaring ceilingwards must have liberated something deep inside her subconscious. Something that first revealed itself as fear and disgust, secondly interest, and now ravening lust. Oh, why do you have this effect on women, Lea? Why can't you be like ordinary men. Your multiple gifts rebound on you.

'You stay here.' I pause in the doorway and prepare for the inevitable. At least I will be protecting Sue from exposure. I might as well look on the bright side. 'Not you.' Wait a minute! The woman is looking at *me*. 'You get out and go about your business.'

'Me?' I say.

'Yes, you.' She turns to Sue. 'You stay here, my dear. I want a word with you.' She shoos me out of the door and closes it in my face. What a carry on. Am I to assume that Sue is to be the repository of the woman's unnatural desires. I drop to my knee and look through the keyhole. Dead in front of me is an eyeball.

'Goodbye,' says the woman's voice.

I get up and go downstairs. Percy is still rearing up like a dog standing on its hind legs after everybody else has left the room. What a stupid prick he is.

CHAPTER SEVEN

In which Sid gets an idea of how to make a bit on the side
and Timmy's girlfriend is got at.

'Then what happened?' says Sid.

'I waited outside the house for twenty minutes and she
didn't come out.'

'Obviously loving every minute of it,' says Sid. 'I read
somewhere that only a woman can really satisfy another
woman.'

'That's wonderful news for us all,' I say. 'I hope word
doesn't get around.'

'I don't tell everybody,' says Sid. 'So you got back on
the round, did you?'

'I couldn't stay there all day. Not with the sun beating
down and my battery getting flat.'

'Very wise,' says Sid. 'It would pay you to concentrate
on the job the whole time and not get involved in these
foolish romantic adventures. There's money to be made
in this game, you know.'

'I sold a hundred and forty yoghurts last week,' I say.
'At half a penny per yoghurt that's—'

'There's a naivety about you that is almost refreshing
in this harsh, commercial age,' interrupts Sid, stopping
his float. 'The trouble is that it's going to leave you skint.
Take a look at this lot.' He opens a suitcase resting on the
crates and I see a dazzling mass of jewellery.

'Blimey, Sid,' I say. 'What do you do? Nip upstairs when they're looking for their purses?'

'I didn't nick it, you berk!' says Sid. 'This is to sell. Why should we only flog Meadowfresh stuff? There's a great chance to make a bit on the side. Look at this for value: a digital, quartz crystal, electronic watch for only fifty-two pence – less than the postage and packing on a normal watch. Press the button and – oh well, you do get the odd one that has slipped through the factory checks.' He throws the watch back into the case and picks up a flashy ring. 'This is the little wonder. It reads your moods. If you're worried it turns yellow, if you're sexy it turns red.'

'What does it mean when it's tin-coloured?' I ask.

'It means the stone has fallen out,' says Sid. 'We're not having a lot of luck, are we? Funny, because the bloke in the pub told me they were some of the finest pieces to pass through his hands.'

'That's true enough,' I say. 'Most of them seem to be in pieces.'

'Don't take the piss,' says Sid. 'That's one of the failings of this country. Too many scoffers, not enough people prepared to have a go. Now, look at this: Jaws underpants. A dirty great set of teeth just where you wouldn't like to find them in real life. Keep the kiddies amused for hours. And look at this: a walking stick that converts into a set of golf clubs or a complete home gardening kit. Dependent on which way you screw in the heads you get a hoe or a number eight iron.'

'That's staggering, Sid,' I say. 'But don't you think it's a little bit dodgy? Mr Claygate expects us to be selling milk and eggs and cream and all that stuff.'

'He's exploiting you,' says Sid. 'I'd do the same in his position. It's dog eat dog in this life. If you don't take, nobody is going to give.'

'But he had such high hopes of you, Sid.'

'I'm going to sell some milk as well!' scolds Sid. 'Blimey, get off my back, will you. I'm only extending the range – in fact I'll probably sell more milk once people get interested. Look at this: a do-it-yourself venetian blind kit. Fits together in no time at all once you've untangled the string.'

'I don't like it, Sid,' I say.

'Well how about a polythene greenhouse? Fold up so that you can carry it in the pocket of your mackintosh. Ultra violet—'

'I mean, I don't like the whole idea,' I say. 'It looks to me like you've got lumbered with another load of rubbish.'

'Rubbish?' says Sid. 'This lot, rubbish? I'll show you. Just stick around and see what the public think.'

'I don't want to, Sid.' I say. 'I've finished my round. I want to get home.'

'You stay here,' says Sid. 'You can't make remarks like that and just walk off.' He starts to hang necklaces round his neck and load his fingers with rings. 'Sid!' I say. 'You look a right berk.'

'Got to show them the merchandise,' says Sid. 'You haven't seen this lot have you?' He opens his shirt and reveals that he is wearing a black nylon peep-hole halter neck bra over his string vest. 'Sexy, huh?'

'Not on you!' I say. 'Sid, this is crazy.'

But he is already opening the front gate and walking

up the garden path. It is all rather symbolic somehow –
shambolic, too. In a fit of madness I follow him. 'This
is where the psychology comes in,' burbles Sid. 'Being
a milkman means that you are accepted by the public.
If I was a common hawker or circular it would be different. People might be a bit surprised. But the magic milk
bottle makes all the difference.' He presses the front
door bell and gives me his 'Clapham's answer to Paul
Newman' smile. 'That and the unquenchable magnetism.'

'Just take the earrings off,' I beg him.

The door opens and a tall, thin bloke wearing a skin-
tight polo neck sweater looks Sid up and down appraisingly. 'Yes, dear?' he says.

'Milko,' says Sid. 'I believe you have already been
persuaded of the virtues of our staple product. May I
suggest that I might be able to show you something else
that could give equal pleasure and satisfaction?'

'Sounds lovely,' says the bloke. 'Why don't you step
inside where we can be a bit more comfy – oh, and leave
that milk outside. I can't stand the stuff. I absolutely
detest cows. Those big floppy udders covered in teats.
They're like washing up gloves, aren't they?'

'Absolutely,' says Sid. 'I'm very grateful I don't have
to see the stuff till it's in a bottle.' He winks at me com-
placently as he steps through the door. 'OK smart arse.
Now do you see how easy it is?'

When I get to the Depot the next morning, a worried
Claygate calls me into his office. 'This new man, Noggett,'
he says. 'How well do you know him?'

'Well,' I say. 'He is my brother-in-law. I find – what's
happened?'

'He appears to be a tranvestite,' says Claygate looking embarrassed. 'You know what that is?'

'Somebody who likes dressing up in bird's clothes,' I say. 'Er – how did this fact come to light?'

'The police were called to a disturbance in Baltimore Street,' says Claygate. 'Apparently he was dancing the hokey cokey on the kitchen table in a bra and pantie set. Some drinking had been going on.'

I shove my mind into overdrive. 'I think you can put the whole incident down to over-enthusiasm,' I say gravely. 'Your clarion call to make a more dramatic use of our sex appeal has gone to his head and other parts. He was probably trying to appeal to everybody at the same time. I think he was very impressed by your ideas and wanted to do everything in his power to make them work.'

Claygate looks distressed. 'So you think that I might have been the involuntary cause of this regrettable incident? Oh dear. I appreciate the man's motives but we can't have our milkmen going about in women's underclothing. Not all the customers would like it.'

'I'll talk to him,' I say. 'I'm certain it will go down better coming from me.'

'Would you?' says Claygate. 'I don't want to trample on the man's initiative but—'

'Don't worry,' I say. 'Leave it to me.'

'It's funny,' says Claygate. 'He got a glowing report from Miss Tromper when he was on his course and she's notoriously hard to satisfy. Still, I think I must pursue a policy of wait and see with Noggett. Exuberance must be tempered with common sense.'

'Exactly my own feelings, Mr Claygate,' I say, practically fluttering my eyelashes. 'I'll do everything in my power to get the point over.'

'Good man, Lea.' Claygate pats me on the shoulder. 'I'm impressed by the way you're shaping up. The girl from the Milk Marketing Board liked the way you handled yourself.'

'Oh good, sir.' That cheers me up a bit after the confirmation of Sid's success with Betty Tromble. 'Well, I'd better be getting along. Mustn't keep the customers waiting.'

I go out under the appreciative glow of Claygate's eyes and feel really chuffed. It makes a change to have someone who actually reckons that I am doing a good job. If I play my cards right I might even get some kind of promotion. And if I got promotion before Sid I would be able to tell him where to get off. That would be nice after all these years.

'There you are. You're a bloody good mate, aren't you? Skiving off and leaving me with that raving poufta.' It is the man himself. Unshaven and with eyes like half-sucked bulls-eyes.

'I didn't know you wanted me to stay, Sid. I thought I'd be cramping your style if I hung around.'

'Oh dear.' Sid leans against a float. 'Don't ever accept a creme de menthe frappé from a complete stranger – especially if it comes in a bone china teacup.'

'Did you sell him anything, Sid?'

Sid snorts. 'He was only interested in opera – you know, that Wagner one called "The Ring". Gawd, the bloody liberties he tried to take. Fancy wanting to try on the bra and pantie set while I was still wearing it. Imagine what it would have done to the material. It could have been stretched out of all recognition.'

'Sid,' I say. 'I don't know quite how to put this, but Mr Claygate is a trifle worried about you. He seems to think that you have a tendency towards the gay.'

'Well I try to put a bright face on things,' says Sid. 'The world can be a pretty grim place sometimes. If you have a smile and a jest for everyone you meet – '

'The homosexual gay,' I say patiently.

'Homosexual?' says Sid. 'You mean, he thinks I'm a ginger? I'll sue the bugger!'

'You must see it from his point of view, Sid,' I say. 'It's not every bloke who goes off to work wearing a peep-hole bra and half a dozen necklaces.'

'You set him right, of course?' says Sid. 'I mean, it's blooming ridiculous.'

'I couldn't,' I say. 'Not without blowing the cover on your little caper. I think the best thing is that you show him in your own inimitable way. When you leave this place you must vindicate yourself.'

'What, in front of everyone?' says Sid. 'Still, you may be right. The time is probably ripe for desperate measures. I will show Claygate beyond any shadow of a doubt that I am not a nancy.'

'Excellent,' I say. 'Now, just take those earrings off and you'll be half way there.'

'Oh dear,' says Sid. 'I forgot about them. I thought Rosie gave me an old-fashioned look this morning.'

When I get home a familiar smell tells me that Mum has either been boiling Dad's smalls or making a steak and kidney pudding – you never know till the top comes off the saucepan, and even then I have had my doubts after the second mouthful.

'Hello, dear,' she says. 'Have a good day? I'm just going to put the kettle on. Do you fancy a cup of tea?'

'No thanks,' I say. 'I've just had one.' This is not strictly true but Mum's tea takes few prisoners.

'There was a telephone message for you this morning. Nicely-spoken girl. Sue something or other. I tried to write it down but your father had taken the biro to mark the *TV Times*.'

'What did she say?' It must have been Sue Danger-field. I don't know any other Sues – I don't know many birds really, not for long.

'She left a number for you to ring after six o'clock. Nine three seven – no, three seven nine – no – '

'Oh no, Mum!' I bleat. 'Don't say you've forgotten it.'

'Special, is she?' says Mum. 'Where did you meet her? What does her father do?'

'I met her in a brothel,' I say. 'Her old man runs it.'

Mum's eagerness to get delumbered of me is beginning to get up my bracket. There was a time when she reckoned Grace Kelly wasn't good enough for me. Now, anyone will do.

'There's no need to be so touchy,' she sniffs. 'I only have your interests at heart – just as I have done since you were a little boy.'

'If you care about my interests, remember that bloom-ing number,' I say.

'I tried to write it down, but the pencil was broken,' says Mum. 'Still, you might be able to read the outline of the letters. I wrote it on the cover of a magazine.'

But when I get in the hall, *Woman's Own* doesn't have a cover. Half the magazine has gone.

'Oh dear,' says Mum. 'Your father must have taken it to the karsi. What a shame. I hope he didn't get as far as the knitting pattern.'

'You ought to buy some blooming bog paper.' I say. 'There's not a magazine in this place that doesn't have some pages torn out of it. Even the library books cop it.'

'You've got to make economies somewhere,' says Mum. 'Anyway, I don't think your father would be able to adjust to toilet tissue after all these years. The texture, you know.'

'Yes,' I say, hurriedly.

'Go and ask him. I think he's still in there. I haven't seen him since dinner.'

'I didn't even know he was home,' I say.

'He wasn't feeling himself today,' says Mum.

'That comes as a surprise,' I say. Dad is the local pocket billiards champion and often falls asleep in front of the telly in mid session.

I go out to the karsi and bang on the door. How unwholesome that the course of true love should have to be conducted in this fashion. 'Hy Yuf,' says a familiar voice.

'Sorry to disturb you, Dad,' I say. 'I'm looking for the—'

The rusty cistern grinds into action and the bolt slides back as the toilet flushes. ' – it doesn't matter.'

'It's all yours,' says Dad stuffing the flaps of his waist coat into the front of his trousers. 'I'd leave it for a few minutes if I were you – '

'Yes, Dad,' I say hurriedly. 'What's that you've got in your hands?'

'Oh that,' says Dad. 'I expect that's—'

'The other hand,' I say. 'That magazine cover.'

'Nice looking woman, that,' says Dad. 'Reminds me of your Aunt Edna. I was going to show it to your mother. Of course this one's got better teeth, but if you put your hand over her mouth – which I've often felt like doing incidentally – '

'Can I borrow it a moment, Dad?' I say. 'Mum wrote a telephone number on it.'

'That was on the back cover,' says Dad. 'I've used that.'

When I get back inside the house, the telephone rings.

'Timothy?' says a familiar upper class voice. 'Thank goodness. I rang the Depot and they said your float was on charge. I tried the house but your mother seemed a little confused so I thought I'd better ring again.'

'Oh, Sue. Smashing,' I say. 'What can I do for you?'

'I was wondering if you'd sponsor me for the Milkmaid of the Year competition at the Festival of Milk.'

'The what?' I say.

'Haven't you heard? Gosh, communications must be absolutely unbelievable. The publicity boys have dreamed it up in combination with the Smithfield Show. Surely you've seen some of the leaflets?'

'Not yet,' I say. 'What do I have to do?'

'Every entrant must be sponsored by a milkman. It's supposed to be from her local area but we can get round that. It ties the whole thing in, you see. "From Udder to 'Uddersfield", get it?'

'Er – yes,' I say. 'Put me down, or whatever you have to do.'

'You have to sign a piece of paper and say what first

attracted me to you. Pretty soppy stuff really. I'm only going in because my boss thinks the department ought to be represented.'

'I'm certain you've got a great chance,' I say. 'I was hoping we'd be able to get together again. What are you doing this evening?'

'I'm tied up this evening,' she says – she gives a little giggle when she says it. 'How about tomorrow? I've got a couple of tickets for the open air opera. It's tremendous fun. You take a hamper and let the music wash all over you while you sip champers.'

'Well,' I say. 'I was tied up tomorrow—'

'I can always get somebody else to come.'

'But I think I can get out of it,' I say hurriedly. 'Yes, ta. That sounds great. Where shall we meet?'

I am a bit surprised to learn that you have to get a train to where they have the opera and that this leaves in the middle of the afternoon. I have to piss round my round and when I get to Victoria station I find that there are a lot of herberts standing around in dinner jackets. I think it must be a Royal Garden Party but when I see Sue she is looking pretty toffed up as well.

'No DJ?' she says.

For a moment I wonder what she is on about. The only DJs I know are of the Emperor Rosko and Tony Heartburn ilk. 'Dinner Jacket,' she explains. 'Oh well, denim never goes out of fashion, I suppose.'

'You mean, all these geezers are going to the opera?' I say. 'Blimey, I'd have worn a tie if I'd known.'

'It doesn't matter,' she says. 'Music sounds the same even if you're naked, doesn't it?' She looks at me in a way that makes me glad that the back of my Y-fronts is not made of an easily combustible material.

'Very much so,' I say. 'Er – allow me to assist you with the hampster – I mean, hamper.' It is stupid but in the presence of all the toffs I start behaving like a mini-herbert. All my natural juices turn into starch. 'Have you got a ticket yet?'

'It's all included in the price of the seats,' she says. 'Don't worry, my aunt is footing the bill.' She smiles gaily and I follow the strands of semi-transparent chiffon towards the barrier. As far as I can make out the train is all first class and we settle into an empty compartment at the back and put the hamper on a rack.

'This is the first time I've seen you since our last little outing,' I say. 'How did you get on with that woman? She seemed a bit kinky to me.'

Sue looks round and snuggles closer to me. 'You're not easily shocked, are you?'

'No,' I say, feeling an interested tingle beginning to curve through my toes.

'It was almost like being hypnotized. When she stared at me I was totally defenceless.'

'Against what?' I say. Another couple come down the corridor and I will them to go past.

'She told me to take all my clothes off and lie on the bed. Then she got a mink glove and began to stroke me. I was frightened and embarrassed at first and then I began to like it.'

'Blimey,' I say. 'Then what happened?'

'She took her clothes off and made me do it to her. She said that if I didn't do it properly she was going to spank me.'

'And did you do it properly?'

'Not to her satisfaction. She made me lie across the bed and then she got the silk cord that was holding up those awful curtains. Do you remember them?'

'Yes, yes,' I say.

'Then she started to whip me with it. Across the bottom and along the back of my thighs.'

'And you let her do it?'

'Well – ' Sue hesitates. 'It was funny but I found it rather exciting. The pain wasn't too bad and I could feel myself getting wet – like when I was with you. When we were sucking each other.' Another couple pause in the doorway as she says 'sucking each other' and then move on. I look after them and then back again as the woman turns and catches my eye. 'Do you remember?'

'Very well,' I say.

'I was in a sort of daze. I couldn't believe it was happening to me. I thought I must be dreaming about someone else. She apologized for hitting me and begged for my forgiveness and then she started licking me – all over with the tip of her tongue.'

'And you liked that?' I say, knowing the answer to my question before I open my mouth.

'I adored it. When she kissed me on the mouth and I felt her naked breasts against mine it seemed the most wonderful and natural thing in the world. Do you think I did wrong?'

'Well,' I say, feeling like I am addressing "Worried, Tooting" in the magazine Dad had in the karsi. 'You weren't, sort of, an active partner, were you?'

'Oh yes, I was,' says Sue, eagerly. 'After a while I was very active. I learned some amazing things about myself. Take last night for instance.'

'Last night?' I say. 'You mean, you saw her again?'

'I couldn't say no. What do you know about Bondage?'

'You mean the films with Roger Moore? She took you to one of those, did she?'

'That's James Bond,' she says. 'I meant tying people up to increase sexual excitement.'

'It's always seemed a bit complicated to me,' I say. 'Supposing you want to blow your nose?'

'It was exquisite,' breathes Sue. 'I don't think I'd better tell you. You probably wouldn't understand.'

'You could try,' I say. 'WaaaaaaaaaH!!!'

'Why did you do that?' says Sue.

'I thought those people were coming into this compartment.'

'There was no need to jump up and down and start strangling yourself. They've probably gone to get the guard.'

'Tell me about your experience,' I say, trying not to sound too eager.

'Well, we both took off all our clothes and then I lay on the bed while she tied me up. Not so it hurt but so that I couldn't move.'

'I wouldn't have let her do that to me,' I say. 'She might have been a bit funny – I mean, even funnier than she obviously was.'

'She probably wouldn't have *wanted* to do it to you,' says Sue. 'Being a man doesn't automatically mean that you're a passport to sexual ecstasy as far as every woman is concerned.' I can't think of a quick answer to that one so I keep my mouth shut and continue to look interested. 'Where was I? says Sue.

'You were tied up on the bed in the altogether,' I say.

'Oh yes,' she says, giving a little smile like she is remembering something nice. 'Then she lay down beside me and started bringing herself off.'

'Bringing herself off?'

'Masturbating. With her fingers at first and then with her fingers and a vibrator. It made a soft whirring noise like when you hear a motorboat across a lake.'

'She must be potty,' I say feeling percy lumber into the vertical at the thought of it all.

'Potty?' Sue looks at me like I am crawling up the outside of the window. 'It was the most sexy thing that has ever happened to me. Being tied up while she was doing that. I was dying to get at her or make love to myself. The frustration was delicious.'

'Er – yes,' I say. 'Well, I suppose – ' I don't want to appear like a square though I can hardly believe my ears. Is it possible that the tide of sexual freedom has washed over me and left me stranded on the beach? Is everybody doing things I had never even thought about? How upsetting. Maybe I had better start remembering all those knots they tried to teach me when I was in the Cubs.

'Then she untied me and made me tie her up. I wanted to make love to her immediately but she said it would be better if we did it her way. So I lay back and closed my eyes – I always do, you know – and started to stroke myself – are you all right?'

'Just changing position,' I say. 'I'm a bit stiff.' I am not kidding either. Down in the groin region it is strictly standing room only.

'But she told me to open my eyes and watch her and myself. Also, to do it very slowly. I didn't use the vibrator, just my fingers. After a while I began to really like it. I could see that she was turned on and that made it even better. Have you ever masturbated with anyone else?' Another couple shiver in horror and hurry past the compartment.

'No,' I whisper, feeling almost guilty. 'No, I haven't.'

'Just shows how sheltered one is,' says Sue. 'We see ourselves as being sexually orientated but in fact it's just the tip of the iceberg.' She looks down into my lap.'Would you like me to suck you?' Percy gives another lurch and for a second I think that my zipper is going to be catapulted from its mooring.

'Please!' I say.

'What does that mean? Please yes or please no?'

'Wait till the train starts,' I say. As if on cue, the guard's whistle makes sweet music in my ear and the train lurches forward in an indifferent imitation of my cock. 'How about the blinds?' I say. But Sue is already bending over my lap. She has just got my zip down when I recognize the first couple who seemed likely to disturb us coming down the corridor. I spring to my feet and snatch the hamper just in time to jam the wickerwork down on my rampant dick. The sensation is not exactly akin to that of being dusted with long-haired velvet.

'In here, Amanda,' says the dinner-jacketed geezer loftily. 'I'm afraid we're going to have to share with the cretin and his friend.'

CHAPTER EIGHT

In which Timmy is taken out of himself in unusual circumstances by a lady called Hermione.

The journey must take two hours and every sodding minute of it I sit with the bloody hamper wedged on top of an enormous hard. What a waste – apart from all the agony. It is like waking up in the morning with a rock cock between your legs and nowhere to direct it except down the lav. Sue sits beside me smiling and looking out of the window and I try not to think of all the things she was doing with my customer. She looks so innocent in her chiffon. If only the other two would push off and discuss *Madam Butterfly* in the buffet car. I could at least tuck myself away.

I still have the same problem when we arrive at a large country house set in rolling grassland and all that caper. My dick is wedged underneath my jeans but it is still jumbo-sized and showing no signs of going down, I wonder if the hamper fouled up the withdrawal mechanism? It is like getting an umbrella jammed as you try to enter a telephone box.

'I don't know about you but I'm famished,' says Sue. 'Shall we find a likely spot and get down to it? Everybody eats before the performance. How does Cosi Fan Tutti grab you?'

'I like any kind of icecream,' I say. 'How about over here behind these bushes?'

I am all for getting stuck into her right away but she is a typical woman. 'Not now!' she says as I try and shove my hand up her skirt 'Why do you have to be so impulsive? Open this bottle. I take it you like Riesling?'

'I don't know,' I say, deciding that it is best to be honest. 'I've never riesled.'

Sue looks at me hard and seriously. 'You have a very strange sense of humour,' she says. 'Ellen never makes jokes.'

Ellen Grant. I see the name staring at me as it did from the note about putting the milk in the fridge. Why did she want it in the fridge? And what about the dripping? I repress a shudder. Control, Lea. The night is young.

'It looks nice,' I say glancing at the bottle and realising that I have made a tiny mistake. 'It's German, is it?'

'Alsatian,' she says.

'Blimey!' She must be joking. It has a heavy yellow colour but surely it can't be –

'From Alsace,' she says. 'On the borders of France and Germany.'

'Oh,' I am unable to keep the relief out of my voice. I mean, those bloody dogs have put the mockers up me since I was a kiddy. I wouldn't fancy patting one, let alone drinking its gypsy's.

I remove the cork – well, in fact it is a bit loose so I push it into the bottle, but it doesn't matter as long as you suck your little finger clean and shove it up the spout and don't mind getting the first pouring up your sleeve. Sue does not say anything but I think she is quietly impressed by the suave way in which I pick the little pieces of cork out of her glass. As I have said before on many occasions: little touches mean a lot to a woman, and I don't mean shoving your hand up the back of her skirt when she's doing the washing up.

Sue unwraps some chicken legs from paper serviettes and the whole occasion begins to reek of high living and good taste. All around us, the grass is littered with people tucking into their nosh and I am reminded of the scene in a layby along the Kingston bypass on a busy Bank Holiday.

'What happens about the opera?' I ask. 'This seems like a blooming great picnic.'

'It's al fresco,' says Sue. 'The whole thing takes place under the stars.'

I rack my brain but for the life of me I can't think of Al Fresco. I remember Al Martino and, of course, the fat bloke Mum liked — Mario Lanza, but this other wop is beyond me. Still, you can't know everything, can you?' Apart from Swan Lake and Les Syphillis I hardly know another opera.

'Lovely spot of grub,' I say, quietly shoving a chicken bone into the lawn so it won't mess the place up. 'Did your aunty knock this up?'

'No,' says Sue. 'I ordered it from Fortnum's. Would you care for a punnet?'

'Not half!' I am just sliding my hand up the inside of her oh-so-cool thigh when she shoves a basket of strawberries into my hand.

'What has got into you?' she says indignantly. 'Have you no control of yourself?'

'I'm sorry,' I say. 'I misunderstood you. Punnet, yes, of course.'

'Ellen was grace personified compared to you,' she says.

'She changed her name, did she?' I ask.

'What are you talking about?'

'You said she was called Grace Personified,' Sue gives me another funny look and I sense that something beautiful may be slipping away fast.

Something that isn't slipping away fast is my old man. There must be something wrong with it. It has got more back bone than a battalion of ghurkas.

'What are you doing?' asks Sue irritably.

'Just getting more comfortable.'

'You're like a monkey,' she says. 'Always playing with yourself.'

'That sounds pretty good coming from you,' I say.

'How petty,' she sneers. 'And how typical of a man. Desperately insecure in the face of any liberated woman. It's not penis envy today, is it? It's fanny fear. You're frightened by the increasing revelation that we're more than well-equipped to look after our own sexual needs. We don't need your thick, insensitive penises.'

'Insensitive?' I say. 'My throbbing friend here is a blooming lighthouse of sensation.'

'I think I'm going off men,' says Sue, holding out her glass. 'Is there any more wine?'

I pour a generous measure up my sleeve and some into her glass and prepare to persuade her that she is wrong. It is getting darker and people are beginning to wander towards the house. No doubt the performance is due to start soon.

'Listen,' I say, deciding to give her the full force of my sophisticated banter. 'Shadows are lengthening and they're not the only things. How about it?'

'How about what?' she says.

'How about trying to recapture the moment of rapture we were about to partake of on the chuffer?' I say. 'When you were bent on parking your lips around my giggle stick. Perhaps I could reintroduce my north and south to your furburger. The rhododendrons beckon.'

Sue looks at me and runs her finger round the rim of her glass. 'I don't know if I feel like it,' she says.

'You felt like it on the train!'

'I know, but that was different.'

'What was different about it?'

'It was hours ago. Talking about Ellen had got me excited.'

'It got me excited as well!' I tell her. 'It still has! Cop a gander at this.'

'Really!' she says. 'Put it away before somebody has a seizure.'

'It's not easy,' I say. 'I think I've done something to it – I think you've done something to it. It won't go down. It's like Birmingham City.'

Sue ignores my amusing little soccer joke and glances round before stretching out her hand. 'Good heavens,' she says. 'It's hot, isn't it?' She looks round again and her eyes settle on the bushes.

I draw closer to her and nuzzle her cheek. 'What do you want me to do with this banana skin?' I ask.

'You could slap it around that thing,' she says.

'Highly amusing,' I say. 'Come on, let's – er shuffle into the shrubbery. I want to show you that there are still some things a bloke can do best.' When I sniff the mixture of perfume and woman smell I feel like sinking my teeth into her there and then.

'We'll miss the curtain going up,' she says.

'I can suggest a substitute,' I breathe.

'You're so coarse,' she sighs. 'Ellen says that men can put their heads between their legs without bending their backs.'

'Stop thinking about Ellen,' I say. 'She's an unhealthy influence.'

I do myself up and pulling Sue to her feet, lead her into the bushes. She is still wittering away but I am pretty certain that once I get her staked out behind the delphiniums she will respond to the old body magic. It is quite dark now and all I can hear is what sounds like the continuous buzzing of a swarm of bees. I hope they are not going to louse everything up. I push my way through a gap in the bushes and draw Sue down beside me. Her breasts are swelling forward and I press my head between them before rising to engulf her lips with my mouth. If she wants to say anything she can't and I gently rock my head from side to side until her tongue meets mine and our kiss becomes a two-way experience. I press her gently back against the grass and slide my hand up inside her skirt. This time there is no resistence. If anything, the pressure of her kiss increases at the moment my fingers brush against the swelling mound in her panties. I slip a finger inside and run it down the moist curls. Uhm. Definitely ripe for the entry of the clefted clit-clobberer. I have already taken off my jacket and I swiftly shed the rest of my threads whilst keeping as much contact with Sue's moving parts as is possible. The night is balmy and a gentle breeze caresses my naked body accompanied by Sue's awakening fingers. If she is still thinking about Ellen Whatsit she does not show it. The bees must have turned in for a spot of kip because the noise has stopped and the only sound is a slight rustle as I ease Sue's panties down to her ankles. She draws her legs up and parts them and I start to play the Moonlight Sonata on her drooling snatch – blimey! I did not expect a full orchestral accompaniment. A spotlight zooms over my head and half a dozen violins start scraping away sounding like they are in the bushes behind us. Hardly have I checked that my heart is still beating than the bush we are performing against starts to move. It is a terrifying experience. One minute I am about to immerse my dick in nether nectar, the next I am crawling across the lawn fast in pursuit of a bush. Things like this don't even happen to you on Clapham Common.

The bush stops and I huddle behind its cover and stare into Sue's worried face. At least she has only left her panties behind. Two more spotlights hit the ground a few feet from us and the orchestra do their nuts. I look up and am horrified to see that there is a huge woman towering over me. She is wearing a long robe and a helmet with horns sprouting from it. 'Lo' she screams. 'I spy a tiny elfin sprite!' I am about to tell her that she has made a mistake when Sue puts her hand over my mouth.

'We've blundered on to the stage!' she hisses.

'What brings you here in this pale guise, oh wanton woodland spirit?' The lady with the horns is belting it out like there is no tomorrow and a bloke dressed in tattered rags jumps over my bush – both of them.

'I know not what thou speakest of!' he rants. 'I am but a poor anchorite, passing through these woods by night.' They both start singing at the tops of their voices and I look around for a way to escape. This is definitely not my cup of tea. I don't even care for the music. I can't see where the audience are without peeping over the bush and when I look around I am blinded by spotlights.

'Then summon all our pixie folk – ' a hand reaches out and pulls me to my feet and I hear a gasp which answers my question about where the audience is. Two girls dressed in wispy costumes take me by the hand and walk me round the stage. It is a good job the costumes are wispy because one of the bits gets snagged on my dick and adds a touch of restrained delicacy to the proceedings. It is certainly needed because my cock is still standing out at right angles to the rest of my body. Maybe I took some of Mum's iron pills in mistake for aspirin.

'Join our revels, dance till dawn – ' More people appear out of the bushes and I find myself part of a large circle of birds and creepy looking blokes who wear slightly more eye shadow. They all start to dance, bringing their knees high in the air. Oh dear, that could be very dicey in my condition. I see Sue gazing up at me in amazement as I start to circle her bush. It is on wheels. I see that when I trip over the wire that is pulling it.

I am just about to bolt into the bushes and only stop running when I reach the bus shelter at the top of Scraggs Lane, when the big bird with the horns and the ragged geezer make a simutaneous explosion of noise and everyone files into the shrubbery to tumultuous applause. I expect to be grabbed by half a dozen coppers but only one languid cove comes up to me.

'Get rid of that, love,' he says, jerking his thumb at my hampton. 'You can only take them one step at a time. Rudolph was a bit naughty slipping you on in the first place.'

'Where is Rudolph?' says one of the male dancers who was prancing round the grass with me. 'Wardrobe have done it again! Look at my sequins. Hanging on by threads. I want somebody's guts!'

'You'll have to make do with cotton like everyone else,' says the first bloke. 'And don't start squawking about Rudi. You know Rudi never watches his first nights.'

'Oh spit!' says the dancer. 'I wish I'd stayed with Sadlers Wells. *They* appreciated me.' He looks at my old man, tosses his head and flounces off.

'There's been a bit of a misunderstanding,' I say. 'If you'll—'

'I know, dear. We didn't get your entrance right. Rudi didn't mention it, you see. We all know his little surprises. Now, what are we going to do about your problem? – ah yes. Hermione!'

A willowy looking bird of about six feet pulls up alongside us and looks me up and down appraisingly. 'First night nerves, dear. Could you straighten him out – or rather, you know what I mean?'

'Poor darling,' says the girl. 'Yes, of course. Michael. We can't have that brutal great thing putting everybody off their chocolate ripples. Come with me, dear heart. Aunty Hermione will take you in hand – should all else fail.'

And she has led me away with the dome of my dongler between her finger and thumb. Dongler but not dangler. The love organ is still presenting arms in impressive fashion. Hermione leads me through the door of a flimsy prefabricated structure, like the maximum security wing of a Southern Irish internment camp and into a small dressing room. 'Hand, mouth or boomps a daisy?' she asks. 'It's a question of which is going to get you back on stage quicker.'

'Actually, I'm a milkman,' I say.

'That doesn't surprise me.' Hermione steps out of a skirt shorter than the Jewish Book of Saints and starts changing the rubber grip on the handle of my cricket bat. 'The last baritone Rudolph engaged came to read the gas meter. Am I doing it too fast?'

'Step against the wall a minute,' I say. 'I have a better idea.'

Pausing only to guide my throbbing dick out of her looks and lingers and into the area of her hot twat, I jerk the aggrieved portion forward and upwards and let nature take its course. Immediately I enter I realize that I have found a friend. Four hundred velvet vices clam round my prick and Hermione knows how to tighten each one of them independently.

'Strangle a mangle!' she gasps. 'This brute is going to take some throttling.'

I don't have time to say anything because I am fighting for the creative future of my love joint. Unless I keep it moving, the compulsive grinding of her pelvis and the dynamic tension of her unmention will turn it into a strip of spaghetti. It is like paddling a canoe through the rapids – unless you go faster than the current the rocks will get you.

'Ooh,' squeals the owner of the elastic grumble. 'At this rate I should be in line for a speaking part.'

'Did you say speaking or squeaking?' I croak. Some of the noises flying around remind me of a film I once saw on the early stages of sinking an oil well. 'Cap that gusher', was I believe, a phrase much used. There is also a persistent throbbing sound which may be the onset of a heart attack or could possibly be caused by the wall we are performing against. This is beginning to come apart at the seams and a whiff of roses mingles with the smell of grease paint and greasy pant.

'Woodland folk stand by for the grotto scene – oops! Sorry' The call boy closes the door with a speed that speaks much for his natural sense of modesty and the reverberation races through my body like a forest fire. A familiar sensation orchestrated and magnified by hours of jumbo-sized inactivity erupts from my throbbing gonads and begins to take physical shape in a churning column of chava lava exploding up my mad mick as if the very richness and thickness of the parboiled fluid was responsible for the delicious slowness of its passage. 'Wheeeeeh!!' Ten million sperm cells lock shoulders against the walls of my hard-pressed prick and I deal out one last desperate thrust to send them out on their way into the promised gland.

'Wumf!' There is a rending noise and the wall behind Hermione drops like the tailgate of a lorry. Unable to restrain myself I lunge forward with Hermione still impaled on my giggle stick like a banger at a barbecue. Her legs are wrapped round my back and her deaf and dumb bears the first brunt of the bushes we crash through. An explosion of blinding light, a quick glimpse of a sea of faces, the horrified expression on the mug of the old bird with the horned helmet and – WOMP! – I am sprawling face down on Hermione, still goolie deep in tonk-throttling snatch. Between my legs I feel a sensation akin to that of an airbed going down in a choppy sea. I turn my head sideways and there is Sue still tucked in behind the moveable bush. The expression on her face combines amazement with something approaching extreme irritation. The warm release is now ricochetting away into the farthest reaches of Hermione's still twitching body and one of my long standing problems is clearly over.

'No hard feelings,' I say to Sue.

CHAPTER NINE

In which Timmy becomes sucked into the vortex of the Balham Self Service Society and gets involved in an unusual competition.

'Blimey! Look at this,' says Dad. 'It's disgusting!'

'Don't wipe it on the tea cosy!' says Mum.

It is breakfast at the Leas. A meal Dad does not always get up in time for. His cakehole is smeared with Golden Shred and Mum's concern is understandable. Dad gives Mum an unpleasant look and wipes his mush on the edge of the tablecloth. 'That better, Miss Manners?' he says. It isn't, because the tablecloth is a plastic one. I close my eyes and imagine that I am back at Windsor Castle – I was snatched by gypsies when very young.

'I wasn't referring to the marmalade,' says Dad, 'though I must say, I don't reckon they make the chunky bits as big as they used to. A few years back they were like bacon rinds.'

'Maybe your mouth has got bigger,' I say.

'That's enough from you, laughing boy,' says Dad. 'I'm surprised to see you gracing us with your presence. Why aren't you out on the job? – and I hasten to add I mean bringing milk to those who have need of it, not to mention a few unwanted delicacies to your own hard-pressed family.'

'It's my late round today, Dad,' I say. 'Surely you're not suggesting I should nick anything?'

'Not nick, save,' says Dad. 'You're not going to tell me you sell out everything on that float? Milk and all that are perishables, aren't they? A lot of it must get bunged away.'

'It doesn't, Dad,' I say.

'It *could* do,' says Dad. 'Use your loaf. A bit of sun on it and that butter could melt away to nothing.'

'I have to account for everything, Dad.'

'Even stuff that gets lifted? I mean, you could be parked at the end of that alley by Holdsworth Road and somebody might nip out of the side door of the boozer and—'

'I'm responsible for anything that gets nicked, Dad.'

'Little Lord Fauntleroy,' sneers Dad. 'You'd see your family starve to death, wouldn't you? Typical of the eurasian of fundamental values that pervades public life today. Decadence and cynicism are rampant. When I was a kiddy I'd have given somebody's right hand to help my old Dad. Look at this paper – it sums the whole thing up. 'Sex shock horror at opera'. They can't even do an opera without bringing sex into it! I remember when they had La Balham on at the Streatham Hill Theatre. Your mother and I didn't go because of the war but . . .'

I tune out Dad's voice and take a discreet decko at the paper. For once it is not open at page three. Through the transparent marmalade stains I read: 'The champagne and caviar audience for the premiere of Rudolph Jagmeister's new opera "Revels of a Midsummer Night" were hardly settled in their twenty-guinea seats before an orgy of full-scale nudity caused lorgnettes to quiver. Naked men in what was described as "an excited condition" ran round the stage and Renalto Scrubbova's first aria "Let little pixie folk come out to play" was sung against the background of naked couples performing explicit sex acts'. Blimey, they do exaggerate. And they have completely left out the bit where the big lady sat down on her helmet. The high note of the show it might have been called. I said that to Sue but she didn't seem to think it was funny. Even allowing for the fact that women have no sense of humour her reaction was disappointing. She said that she was hurt about me having if off with Hermione – she was hurt: Once the last spurt of heady ecstasy had disappeared up the swannee, my condition was more akin to rupture than rapture. You could have knitted my old man into a floppy pullover. In fact, I think Sue really was jealous. It is ridiculous but the moods of women are very changeable. If you lap them up they don't want to know but if they catch you in a mood of amorous dalliance with their best friend's grumble then they can begin to reckon you passionately. Of course, passion in a bird is not always revealed in a sexual sense – not directly. Sue expressed herself by kicking me in the crutch as soon as that article was revealed. I would have preferred something less demonstrative myself but it is nice to know that people care.

'. . ."Il Travesty",' says Dad. 'That was another one they did. Everybody clothed the whole way through it – and why not, I'd like to know? Audiences didn't need filthy smut in those days. We were happy with simple things. A good tune well sung: "Only a rose I give you-u-u-u – " '

'Yes dear,' says Mum. 'Would you like some—'

' – "I'd bring along a smile and a song for anyone. But only a rose for you-u-u- – '. They don't compose songs like that these days.'

'Can I have that in writing?' I say.

Despite the fact that the theatre critic of Dad's paper finds 'Revels of a Midsummer Night': 'a cataclysmic blend of the what might have been and the what is to be, suffused with a soft wanton poetry all its own,' I am not sorry to get back to my float and the problems of putting Meadowfresh on the map. We get a bonus for bringing in new customers but so do all the local dairies. The competition is thus bitter to put it mildly – ho, ho. One of the nastiest nerks in the neighbourhood is the geezer from Universal Dairies who punched Sid up the throat.

Despite the fact that nobody who belts Sid can be all bad this bloke comes close. Not only is he very free with his love lolly but he puts about a lot of nasty rumours concerning Meadowfresh: they are on the point of going bankrupt so one might as well change now rather than suddenly be without milk, local health inspectors are not satisfied with the bottle-washing arrangements, Mrs Phillips at Number 46 found a centipede in her orange juice etc, etc. He is a right stirrer – and not least of all with the giggle stick. Being a window cleaner was tough enough but being a milkman is even rougher because you have to go through the card every day – I mean, they have a daily chance to pop out and grab you. Sometimes, it is like leaving milk outside a spider's web. You tiptoe up to the front door feeling that eyes are watching you through the letterbox. A careless chink from the empties and the hampton-starved bint on the other side will be alerted to your presence. Honestly, I can tell you one thing for definite – the women of Great Britain are not getting enough. If you don't believe me, ask your old lady – or for a more honest reply, ask somebody else's old lady. She will give it to you straight – provided, usually, that you give it to her back in the same condition.

A practical example of this state of affairs – appropriate choice of phrase – is afforded by my contact with the Balham Self Service Society. My first brush with them takes place on a hot afternoon when the bottle tops are starting to curve upwards and the tar sticks to the wheels of my float. It has been hot for days and the sight of birds wearing practically nothing is no novelty to me. I have nearly finished my round and am eager to clock off and get home to a cold bath – even if it does mean the sweat of moving the coal out.

'Yoo hoo. Milkman!' The bird is calling to me from across the street and is not one of my regulars. Oh well, I suppose I had better show willing.

'Yes ma'am,' I say, coaxing my sticky limbs towards the garden gate. 'What can I do you for?'

As I get nearer I see that she appears to be wearing a sheet and sandals. Oh well, nothing too unusual about that. 'I don't know what's happened to our milkman,' she says looking up the street. 'I don't think we can wait any longer. Fourteen pints please. Can you manage that?'

'Certainly, ma'am,' I say. 'Delighted to oblige. At Meadowfresh we always carry a bit extra.'

The bird reacts to this harmless statement and another appears in the doorway behind her. She is wearing the bottom half of a bikini. At first I think she is wearing the top half too but then I realize that I am looking at the bits that have not caught the sun – few bikinis have large nipple patterns on them. It is a bit saucy but the sun has a funny effect on some people. They read about topless beaches at St Tropez and reckon they can start behaving like that in Balham. No reason why they can't, I suppose.

'Meadowfresh to the rescue,' says the first bird.

'Poor dear,' says the second bird. 'Doesn't he look hot?'

'Anything else?' I say, grabbing as much milk as I can.

'Come and have a dip,' says the second bird.

'Oh well,' I say, thinking about it. 'You got a pool, have you?'

'Just a little one,' says the bird. 'But it's better than nothing. You can get cool.'

I am in the house now and there is a funny pong which I think is incense. I don't care for it myself but I have found that people who use it are usually of what you might call liberated tendencies. 'Where do you want the milk?' I say.

'In the kitchen,' says the second bird. 'Down the end of the corridor.' She stands against the wall so that I have to brush past her knockers. 'Sorry,' I say.

'That's all right,' she says. 'We must try it again some time.'

Something tells me that I have not stumbled upon the local Salvation Army headquarters. There is another bird in the kitchen and she is completely starkers. She has just opened a tin of Carnation milk – a blob of which has been fortunate enough to collide with her knockers. As I look at her, the topless bint comes up behind me and bends her head to lick the milk off her mate's manchesters. I clear my throat and concentrate on putting the milk down without dropping any of the bottles.

'I'm trying to persuade him to stay for a swim,' says Topless.

'Good idea,' says Starkers, running her eyes over me

like my body comes equipped with rails. 'We're short of a couple of members.' They both have a little laugh at that and I look through the kitchen window to the back garden. This is pocket handkerchief size with a kiddies' paddling pool in the middle of it.

'Is that it?' I say. 'It's not exactly Olympic size, is it?'

'It depends on your sport,' says Topless. 'I don't think you probably know about us?'

'Not exactly,' I say.

'We're the Balham Self Service Society. We help ourselves.' She flicks her hand against the front of my apron in a gesture that some might consider provocative. 'Take your clothes off and join us.'

As is my simple, British, uptight way I begin to feel nervous the moment a bird takes the initative. ' – Er – it's a bit difficult,' I splutter. 'My float's in the sun and I ought to—'

'Move it,' interrupts Topless.

'Move it!' echoes Starkers. She twitches her bum and then starts to circle the kitchen clicking her fingers and moving her bum a whole lot more.

'The Balham Self Service Society exists to help people act out their fantasies,' says Topless. 'That's putting it broadly. Some people don't even know what a fantasy is.'

'We give them ideas,' says Starkers. This does not come as a big surprise to me and I wonder if it is just the heat in the kitchen that is making me sweat.

'Fantasies can take many forms,' says Topless. 'Some of them are sheer escapism – the helicopter landing on the front lawn and an Arab sheik getting out. But many are much more closely related to the day to day reality of a woman's existence. She spends most of the time in the kitchen so that's where her fantasies take place. I love pressing myself against the cool front of the fridge so that the maker's name plate tickles my nipples and imagining a man's hand sliding up between my legs.' She spread-eagles herself against the large white surface of the fridge and I watch the muscles on the back of her thighs tighten and her bum jut out appealingly.

'Like this?' I say. I slide my hand up from behind the knee and pluck at the curls peeping out of her panties. Up over the smooth curve and then inside the panties and down to the hot, moist furrow. I grab a handful and push and Topless squirms with pleasure.

'I like the ironing board,' purrs Starkers who has come up behind me and slid her arms round my waist. 'Every time I'm doing the ironing I imagine laying face down on the board. The cover is still warm from the iron. My legs are pulled apart and hang down so that my toes brush against the floor . . .' While she is talking, her fingers move expertly to the front of my trousers and pull down the zip. Percy is a hard bar of flesh against my stomach and her mit closes about him as if grasping the handle of a sword: '. . . and then I feel it sliding into me as if it's never going to stop. Inch after inch of hot, throbbing cock . . .'

She does have a way with words, doesn't she? Small wonder that a few million sperm cells slightly aft of my shaft start to agitate like snow flakes in a shaken paperweight. The cleft of Topless's bum pulsates temptingly in front of me and I release my belt and pull down my pants so that percy has more freedom. As if reading my mind, Starkers pushes him forward and down so that he rubs against the silken material that guards the entrance to Topless's snatch. Her hands go down and release two strings at the side of her panties so that they flutter to the ground. Now, the dome of my dick is rubbing against her juicy pleasure pot. She closes her legs tight and slides her hand down so that she can squeeze my nob with her fingers and push it hard against her twat. I am now a sandwich filling between her and Starkers who is gently massaging my orchestras.

'What's *your* fantasy?' breathes my testicle-tugging chum.

'This'll do until I think of something,' I grunt.

'I like it bending down, too,' says Topless. 'I like to imagine that when I'm getting something out of the vegetable drawer somebody pushes me forward into the potatoes and pins me so I can't move . . .'

She bends down and by an amazing coincidence my old man is quivering against her open passion purse. Do I slip or does Starkers give me a little push? Either way it doesn't matter because the result is the same – half a foot of hampton willowing into the velvet void like a snake swimming up a narrow creek. I reach forward and feel the heavy fruit of the noble knockers weighing down my palms. Hey ho, this beats plugging your float into the charging machine any day. At moments like this it seems ridiculous that the Timothy Lea set only comes equipped with one prick. Starkers obviously agrees with me because when I glance back it is to see that she has left my goolies for a cucumber which she is withdrawing from the fridge – there are a pile of them in there.

'The coolest fuck since Jack Frost,' she says reaching for the vegetable knife. 'Just dip in sour cream and – eh voila!'

I look away while she gets to work with the knife because it gives percy uncomfortable twinges. When I glance back she is sitting on the edge of a chair with her legs apart and her feet stretched out. Her head is tilted back in satisfaction and her position reminds me of that of a cellist playing herself instead of her instrument. In and out goes the cucumber and it could give you a complex when you saw how much disappeared. I have my hands firmly round Topless's belly and I am making sure that she can't wriggle away from me as I build up the thrusts.

'What's happened to the tea?' The bird in the sheet who first hailed me, appears in the doorway followed by an enormous bearded spade who is gleaming with sweat. 'Grant has just finished serving community needs and he needs refreshment.'

'You can say that again, Mabel,' says the spade, rolling his eyes. 'Call me Mr Wish Fulfilment.' I glance down towards where most of the sweat is running and nearly shunt Topless into the cooker. The cream-spattered dongler dangling below waist level looks like a demolition ball or the knotted fist of a well-developed fourteen-year-old. If I have caught it at an off-duty moment, who dares to think of the full erectile potential of this princely part? I reckon that if you fitted it into a golf bag you would have to carry the clubs under your arm.

'I'm just putting the kettle on,' says Starkers, gritting her teeth for a grandstand finish. 'Anybody fancy a cucumber sandwich?'

'It's going to be more like puree by the time you've finished,' says Topless peering between her legs. She reaches up and suddenly darts a finger where no lady has ever darted a finger before. 'Eek!' The effect whether intended or not is instantaneous. Half a level tablespoon of seminal fluid leaves my body as if shot by a gun and Topless jerks forward with my swollen dome ensuring that we travel together. Fortunately, she has removed her finger as the barrier between pleasure and pain has always been firmly established as far as I am concerned. For a second or two I feel like a piece of paper that has been held against an electric fan and then the honey flows in slow, shuddering, juddering spurts of tingling pleasure.

'Grant is our coalman,' explains the woman in the sheet.

'Coalman, hole man,' says the spade with a laugh. 'Jeeze, the totty in this place really works you over man.' He fills a kettle with water and puts it on the gas, shaking his head. Mabel reaches into a cupboard and brings out a tea caddy. Starkers bites the end off her cucumber and starts setting out cups and saucers on a tray and suddenly everything is getting quite domesticated. If it wasn't for the nudity and the noise when I come apart from Topless I would think that I really had dropped in for a cup of tea.

'Thank goodness you've joined the club,' says Mabel, pleasantly. 'We do need more men. An awful lot falls on Grant.'

'Because I'm black,' grins Grant. 'Every girl wants to try it once.'

'And when she's tried it once she wants to try it again,' says Starkers giving his ebony love trunk an affectionate squeeze and brushing it against her creamy snatch. 'Don't forget your old friends.' She is on the point of tucking him away when the kettle boils and Mabel fills the teapot. 'Take the tea round with Grant,' she says to me. 'He'll show you the lay of the land.'

'The lays of the land, buddy,' says Grant putting sugar

125

on the tray. 'You ain't seen so many women getting their rocks off.'

'That was nice,' says Topless, running her hand up my thigh 'I'll see you later at the cluster fuck.'

I smile pleasantly at her little joke and open the door for Grant. He is certainly better built than the average British motor car, with slabs of muscle thicker than the tray he is carrying.

'The room on the left,' he says.

'Tea up!' I shout cheerfully. It is not the only thing. A whippet-thin geezer is serving dick to a lady sitting on the television set. She seems to like it in the mouth and in the other place as well to judge by the way she swings backwards and forwards.

'Upstairs, Downstairs,' says Grant. 'You can see she's a telly addict.'

'Don't let it get cold,' I say putting down a couple of cups. 'You must be kidding,' says the bloke. 'The sun will cool down before this lot.'

'Where do all these women come from?' I ask as we go out. 'Around,' says Grant. 'Their husbands think it's a kind of Womens Institute. All de girls sitt'n aroun' an' knittin' and listening to lectures on basket weaving.' He laughs and starts up the stairs. The ceiling to the left is shaking in time with a loud thumping noise and a thin rain of plaster is falling. 'They get weavin' all right,' grins Grant. There is a noise like two hippos fighting over a water hole and when I poke my head round the bath-room door it is to find that the bath contains two birds and a bloke wearing all his clothes. 'I only came to clean the windows,' he says. 'You haven't got a bath bun, have you?'

'It's funny,' I say as we go out. 'That bloke reminded me of Robin Askwith.'

'It's difficult to say,' says Grant. 'I never seen him with his clothes on.'

Upstairs, the noise is incredible. Like a torture test for bedsprings or a gang of blokes trying to tenderize elephant steaks with baseball bats. The cups of tea are slopping into the saucers with the vibration.

'Sounds like Big Jeff is getting into his stride,' grunts Grant. 'This is where the girls like to dress up a bit.' I see what he means when the door is opened. I don't know if you ever take a gander at those shops which sell fancy underwear – if you are like me you take a quick peep before somebody reckons that you are kinky – but the birds in the bedroom have got all the kit. No holes barred you might say. The bodies are nothing to threaten Raquel Welch with but the fishnet stocking could clean up every cod off Iceland and there are enough satin bras to set up the fruit for a Lord Mayor's banquet. Big Jeff is humping some old boiler who couldn't touch her feet round his back if you gave her ten quid to try. Her fat little thighs tremble in the air and she is laughing and crying like a crazy woman. Her breasts have left her built-up bra and are floating round her chest like a bucket of blancmange. A pair of scarlet lace-trimmed panties still dangle from one of her toes. Two other birds are sharing a double-ended dildo and it could be said that a mood of easy intimacy prevails.

'It's amazing what goes on,' I say. 'A quiet street in Clapham and yet you could be – ' I break off as I realize that I can't think of anywhere.

'In your imagination,' prompts Grant. 'Nothing's real

about here. I'm not real, I came to deliver de coal the first time I came here. This is as much of a fantasy for me as it is for them.'

The bird on the bed comes and her feet drop to bed level as she rides out her orgasm. Big Jeff lets her enjoy it and then withdraws slowly. I notice that his hampton is still in full working order. Glistening like a giant-size stick of rock with the pattern sucked off.

'He's saving himself for the grand finale,' says Grant.

'Grand finale?' I say.

'It's a bit like a gang bang, man,' says Grant. 'But instead of us going through a chick, all the chicks go through us. They try to make us come. The art is to hold on to your seed for as long as you can. If you wilt then you're out whether you've shot you're load or you're too knackered to keep it up. Last to come is Stud of the Month. The ladies have their own self-destructive little competition. The chick who can trigger off the most fellers gets a prize.'

'And what's that?' I ask.

'First crack at me during the next session of the society,' says Grant modestly. 'Mostly they go it alone so it's not too bad but when they pair up you can have problems. The lesbians are the worst. They want to make you come so that they can prove that they could do it like falling off a log if they really wanted to. You know what I mean?'

'Er – yes,' I say, watching the naked lady who is greasing the bannister with what looks like half a pound of marge. Surely she can't be – 'Wheeeeeeh!' She has. And on to the curiously shaped knob at the bottom, too. I wondered why it was placed in that position. I must get out of this madhouse. Much of what is happening borders on the unwholesome. I will finish crashing the Rosie Lea, retrieve my clobber, say a polite ta and scarper over the fence at the end of the garden. I am prepared to go through so much for Meadowfresh but—

'What are you doing here?' The words come from the large fuzz-fringed cakehole of Desperate Dan, Sid's mate from Universal Dairies. He seems to be filling the hall like he has been hammered into it to keep the walls apart and the expression on his face would make James Bond burst into tears. I look over my shoulder hopefully but it is clear that he is talking to me.

'Hi,' I say, wishing my voice hadn't decided to break at that moment. 'They wanted some milk so I—'

'This is my territory.' Desperate Dan steps forward and puts a menacing hand on the bannister. Unfortunately, the bird has just started greasing it again and he slips and stumbles. I sense that this does nothing to improve his temper and turn to Grant for support – before I end up with the kind that needs a harness to keep it in place.

'Ah, there you all are. You've arrived just in time, Dan.' Mabel comes out of the kitchen rubbing her hands on a Kleenex. 'Yoo hoo, girls. It's time for our fantasy fornication fest.'

'Er—hem,' I murmur. 'Time I was getting along. I'll drop by for the empties on – on second thoughts you can hang on to them. They're great for soaking paint brushes or—'

'Yellow, huh?' sneers Desperate Dan. 'When it comes to a showdown you're off like a super-charged piss. No wonder Meadowfresh are such a load of wankers.' A crowd of clearly excited birds are beginning to assemble in the hall and it is clear that Desperate Dan's words cannot go unanswered. 'We can hold our own with anybody,' I say looking him straight in the second shirt button.

Dan laughs scornfully. 'Just what I said. You have to hold your own. Nobody else is going to. Either that or you need a pair of splints.' He turns to the birds. 'Come to Universal, girls. That's where the action is.'

'No aggravation, boys,' says Mabel, wagging a finger. 'Why don't you settle this thing like men?'

This suggestion meets with a resounding chorus of approval from the surrounding birds and before I can shout for help I am swept through the door into the living room. The furniture has been pushed back against the wall and a large sheepskin rug covers the centre of the room. I find myself standing back to back in the centre of the room with Grant, Big Jeff, the bloke who was dishing it out on the telly and another herbert who looks as scared as I do. Desperate Dan is stripping off his clobber to reveal a beer belly and a dongler like one of those things you hang on to in the tube.

About twenty birds divide their attention between us and Mabel, who is squinting at a stop watch, says, 'Right! Ready, steady, gonads!'

Like a pack of hounds they are on us. I have not seen anything like it since the start of the Olympic marathon – which I would willingly be running in. A solid – well, solid in places – wall of female flesh drives us back to back with a stinging slap. One woman's north and south plunders my lips whilst a pair of hands grabs my dick giving one of the blokes a blow job whilst her mate licks like it is the village pump. I stagger back and stumble over a bird who is already down on her hands and knees giving one the blokes a blow job whilst her mate licks his orchestras. I don't have much time to look because no sooner have my shoulders touched the ground than I receive a mouthful of berkeley from an anonymous donor known to me only by the mole in her fuzz and the high pitched squeaks she lets out while she presses down with her snatch. Her knees are on either side of my nut and I have less chance of getting up than a mad elephant in a mink farm. Whilst I fight for breath a lot of that very same commodity is being deployed around my mad mick. At a guess – since I can't see through the lady currently brillo-padding my teds – I would say that there were two pairs of lips engaged in lifting my giggle stick into the vertical. What a sensation. It is like sticking it in a jar of butterflies.

At the rate I am going – or rather, the rate I am being gone over I would reckon that my chances in this trial of strength were thinner than a whippet's twinkle, but deliverance arrives in the shape of the sad-faced bloke who collapses after a stand up quickie against the electric fire – quite who turned it on is something I never find out. This sets the seal for what is to follow. That it is a dirty contest goes without saying, but the lengths that some of the contestants go to are not just the ones being candle-snuffed by cakeholes and cunts as soon as they rise above the level of the carpet pile.

After a few lunges I get smart. Big Jeff, Grant and Desperate are sorting out most of the action and I move round the rug like a hepped up caterpillar delicately darting my tongue where it will earn a favourable response but wriggling percy away from any permanent entanglement. The scene on the rug is like a game of spillikins played with earth worms and I have never had a more detailed gander at the female anatomy. I used to think that all fannies were the same but when you are pressed up against a roomful of them you realize how wrong this is. Some of them are clefts like the notch in a creamless doughnut. Some seem to be worn outside the body – I think of sea anemones and underwater plants with waving tendrils. Some are like half-opened flowers responding to the morning sun. Some are covered in hair so thick that you can hardly see them – they seem like a shadowy pattern on a caterpillar's back. Others are surrounded by the merest wisps of sandy coloured candy floss. Some stick their tongues out at you. Some bulge like well-stacked wallets.

'Urrrrrrr!' That was the epilogue for the bloke who was on the tele – having it off on top of the telly. There is some argument as to whether the score should be awarded to the bird who was buffing his bollocks or the one who was clambering up his slippery pole and doing more slipping than climbing. It was definitely a team effort as the four bints pinning down his arms and legs would be swift to acknowledge. I leave a heated discussion taking place over the poor sod's desemerized dongler and try and crawl behind a settee.

'No you don't!' A slippery little bird with a body like a skinned rabbit grabs hold of my leg and tries to pull me back on the rug. I feel like a wrestler struggling to make the safety of the ropes. She slips her hand between my legs and launches herself up my body so that she is nuzzing my shoulder. 'You don't want to get away, do you?' I don't know what she is doing to the bit behind my flowers and frolics but it clearly has a very positive effect on the hampton. I can feel this by the pressure against the rug. Perhaps I have been using the wrong tactics. If I can tuck percy away in this little charmer he may be safe from the rest of them. I let the bird transfer her lips to my mouth and turn her light body over so that I can break her half nelson on my hampton. Scrambling between her legs I bend them back so that her feet are hanging over her shoulders and lay my cock against her belly. I press it down and my knob rubs against her fuzz and suddenly dives into her twat like a rabbit into its hole. A shuddering groan behind me comes from Big Jeff who has over-responded to three ladies who have been tickling his cluster with ostrich feathers. The things they get up to, some of them. That leaves two down and three to play – Grant, Desperate and myself. Grant is not holding anything back and has two birds lying on top of each other with their thighs overlapping. A few thrusts in one and then he rises up and gives the other a going-over. Other birds are flopping about him and trying to get their hands on his dick but it is like trying to lassoo a conger eel. Desperate has taken cover in Mabel – something she offers a lot of. She reminds me of a welsh dresser stacked with suet puddings. Desperate is in her like a pencil stuck in a mound of plasticine and is lashing out with his elbows in a very unsporting fashion. He is definitely the winning type, not prepared to abide by the mood of light-hearted fivolity that prevails amongst the rest of the contestants. The bird who has turned the hair dryer on my orchestras, for instance – ooh! Madam, please! What a strange sensation – especially when I get a blast up the khyber. That can't be in the Marquess of

133

Queensberry rules. I lunge forward and bash into the fire irons – despite the fact that there is an electric fire, Mabel has a little shovel, a brush and a pair of tongs.

'WOWWWWHHHHH!!!' That sounds like Grant and – yes! the contest has taken a dramatic and unexpected turn. Even as I watch I see the giant black hampton blunder into an unaccommodating wall of flesh and collapse like a stricken airship. Timber! Stand by with the Kleenex and a steel comb for the sheepskin rug. Now it is only Desperate and me and the honour of Meadowfresh is at stake – not to mention the customers I will be able to pull in if I can best the beast. I try to think of empty milk bottles and dented yoghurt packs but it is not easy to keep my mind off the business at hand. Half the birds in the room seem to be pressed up against me and they are feeling my action man kit like they are testing it for ripeness. The bird nursing my dick has the drawing power of a Dyno-rod demonstrator and it seems likely that a few million sperm cells will be passing out shortly before I do. There is no time to lose. I turn my head with difficulty and see that Desperate is now on his back with Mabel balancing on the thick shaft of his hampton. His balls bounce together like those perpetual motion jobs that hang from pieces of string. How vulnerable they look. I stretch out my hand to get a better grip on the rug and my fingers blunder into the coal tongs. Surely I couldn't – ? or could I? No sooner has the idea occurred to me than I find my fingers closing round the tongs as if programmed by some mystic force – Claygate, maybe; or perhaps Sid. After all, Desperate did belt him. I insinuate my arm between a pair of legs, over another body and there we are. The curved bits of the tongs strategic-

ally placed to close round the swinging goolies. Just a tiny squeeze and – 'YOOOOWWWWWWHHHHH!!!!'
Oh well, it was his fault. If he hadn't lashed out and caught me up the backside I wouldn't have forgotten what I was doing and squeezed so hard.

CHAPTER TEN

In which Timmy is interrupted whilst getting to grips with a new customer.

'So you're not going back to defend your title?' says Sid.

'Definitely not,' I say. 'It's not my cup of tea. If I hadn't seen your mate going off in the ambulance I would have thought I'd dreamed the whole thing.'

'He's going to love you when he comes out,' says Sid.

'He thinks it's an accident,' I say. 'Somebody said they trod on the tongs.'

'Very handy,' says Sid. 'That cost you a bit, didn't it?'

'A bit of the other,' I say. "It's amazing how you can keep it up once you get into your stride.'

'I wouldn't know about that,' says Sid condescendingly. 'I'm concentrating on selling. With me the customer comes first.'

'They usually do with me,' I say. 'I mean, it leaves a better impression, doesn't it? Once I've made them happy I—'

'Must you go on?' says Sid witheringly. 'I'm talking about flogging milk. I've introduced some dynamic new selling ploys.'

'I heard about that, Sid,' I say 'Frankly, I thought it was a bit daft. Who wants to find a plastic whistle at the bottom of their milk?'

'It wasn't in all the bottles,' says Sid. 'Just a selected

few. A special mystery prize for lucky Meadowfresh customers.'

'Not much of a mystery when there's a bloody great hole in the foil,' I say.

'It could have been tits,' says Sid.

'Not unless they were scuba diving in the milk,' I say. 'Anyway, it can't be very hygienic.'

'You're just like bleeding Claygate,' moans Sid. 'You'd stifle all initiative, wouldn't you? You're a microcosm of the national malaise.'

'Watch your language,' I say. 'There are ladies present.'

'Not many around here,' says Sid. 'The class of bird you get in here is strictly on the make.'

We have forsaken the Highwayman and are in the public bar of the Bricklayer's Arms. There are a few middle-aged birds dotted about but they look pretty harmless to me. I make this observation to Sid who shakes his head full of the wisdom of many summers and a correspondence course in book-keeping – he thought it was book making. 'They're lonely,' he says. 'They come here for companionship. All that "hello, George. Hello, Gladys. Has Anthea been in today?" That's them shrieking out for sexual fulfilment.'

'They're very discreet about it,' I say.

'It's in their nature,' says Sid. 'If it wasn't they'd be down the bingo like everyone else. Still, from what I hear your average old age pensioner is a lousy poke so it may be more than middle class genitality.'

'Or even gentility,' I observe.

'Or even that,' says Sid. 'Places like this can be a rich source of customers. These kind of birds are two stagers. They don't come right out and ask you home for a cup of Ovaltine. They say they've decided to change their milkman because the last one was so unreliable – that means he wouldn't come across with a bit of the other – and invite you to call on them professionally. *Then* they invite you in for a cup of Ovaltine.'

'This has happened to you has it Sid?'

'Scores of times. That's why my round covers such a large area.'

'And why you frequently have to push your float back to the Depot with a flat battery.'

'Exactly. Honestly, that geezer Claygate doesn't know what I go through for his blooming dairy. And when I say go through—'

I tune out Sid's voice because I have just copped a gander of a bird that has come into the snug – you can just see it round the corner of the partition that separates the haves from the have nots. She is very handsome and at first I think she has slipped in for a packet of fags. Then I see the gin and tonic – ice and lemon, of course – sliding across, and her neat little cakehole descending to the rim of the glass.

'How's that bird of yours?' says Sid. 'Getting it regular, are you?'

'I haven't seen her for a while,' I say, still watching the bird in the snug. I know that if I stare at her long enough she will feel the vibrations and have to look. I read it in an advertisement somewhere.

'Not surprising,' says Sid. 'If she fancied the opera, you clearly weren't her type. What was it like?'

'Oh, like you see on the telly sometimes,' I say. 'Everybody bursting out of their costumes and singing like they were calling for help.'

'I don't mean the bloody opera!' says Sid. 'I mean the bird. Was she good with it?'

'Oh, Sue,' I say. 'Yeh – well – you – know—'

'You mean, you never had her,' says Sid. 'I can tell by the way you keep swallowing your spit. Why don't you admit it?'

'Because you never give me the chance to say anything, that's bleeding why!' I tell him. 'There's more to a relationship than just banging your willy up her snatch, you know. When I really fancy a bird I'm more interested in finding out if we're mentally attuned.'

'What a load of cobblers,' says Sid. 'You couldn't mentally attune a transistor radio. You're interested in the same thing as I am: velvet fundament squeezing the natural juices out of your hampton.'

Sid can be very coarse sometimes but that is not the only reason I keep my eyes peeled in the direction of the snug. The bird must look my way soon. She can't keep staring into her gin like she is looking for the Loch Ness monster. Maybe she saw *Jaws* and is not taking any chances. Ah! At last. She glances round the rest of the pub and I flask my pearlies at her. Wow! That was a definite smile or my name isn't Septimus Offbrake. 'Ah hem, Sid,' I say. 'I'm just going to have a Jimmy Riddle.' I pause. 'And yes, I would like another pint. Thank you.'

'I don't think you should have another one,' says Sid. 'It's going straight through you. You just had a piss.'

I don't hang about to answer but scarper out of the bar and down the corridor. Pausing only to run a comb through my barnet and make sure that I don't have any pieces of crisp round my cakehole I prepare to bolt into the snug. Sid did me a favour by mentioning Sue. She has not exactly been arduous in her pursuit of me since the evening at the opera and I keep wondering if she is getting all the satisfaction she needs with Ellen Grant and her naughty ways. It does not do a lot for your self esteem when the bird you fancy reckons another bloke, but when she reckons another bird – well, you might as well jack it in and rearrange your stamp collection. What I need is a meaningful relationship with a bird who fancies me rigid – or in any other condition – to wash the memory of Sue away and prove that I am still capable of pulling a bird who is not a member of the Balham Self Service Society.

I take a deep breath and walk into the snug. The bird is sitting on a stool against the bar and her skirt rides up attractively around her thigh. She smoothes it down gracefully with long, elegant fingers and smiles a welcome.

'The answer to my unspoken prayer,' she husks. 'Do you by any chance have a light?' Her voice is soft and posh and she raises a snout to her glistening lips and widens her mince pies hopefully.

I don't have a light because I reckon anyone that smokes must be round the twist but it is not a point of view that I judge it politic to air at this moment in time. The lady is old enough to know what she is doing and I might as well play along with this small vice in the hope that she has bigger and better ones.

'One moment,' I say with professional cool and reach round the partition to where the book match dispenser is resting on the counter of the saloon bar.

'Here! What do you think you're doing?' says the landlord who has a face like a bull terrier disappointed in love.

'Just setting this lady alight – I mean, getting this lady a light,' I correct myself.

'You weren't trying to sneak off with the collecting box by any chance? The Doctor Barnardo's went last week.'

'How dare you!' I mean, what a blooming marvellous way to start a romance. Accused of nicking a pile of lousy book matches. Is it something about my face? The Archbishop of Canterbury never seems to have this trouble.

'I asked the gentleman for a light, George,' says the bird severely. 'He had no intention of taking your silly matches.'

'Exactly,' I say. 'You want to be more careful before you start making accusations.'

The bird smiles at me sympathetically and the landlord goes away mumbling and shaking his head. 'There was no excuse for him to speak to you like that,' she says, lowering her voice. 'I think he's been having a few problems with his wife and that's made him very disgruntled.' She pushes her lips forward and I set fire to her cigarette. Our eyes meet and I hold her glance while I coolly shake the match dead and nonchalantly toss it into her drink.

'Oh,' I say. 'Oh dear – er, yes.' I remove the match and watch the little black bits sink to the bottom of the glass. Fortunately they are hidden by the slice of lemon.

'Thank you,' says the bird. 'You're not a habitué, are you?'

Frankly, I am not used to birds enquiring after my religious views within seconds of us meeting so the question rather throws me. 'Er – no,' I say. 'Just straightforward C of E.'

She looks puzzled for a moment and then gives a little laugh. 'Oh yes, delightful.'

'It's all right,' I say. 'Mind you, I don't go very often.'

'Quite.' She raises her glass to her lips and puts it down again. 'Tell me, what do you do?'

'I'm a milkman,' I say.

It is amazing but her eyes definitely light up. Sid must be right. 'A milkman,' she repeats like I have said I am Henry Kissinger. 'How fortuitous. Do you deliver on Sundays?'

'Definitely,' I say. 'It's a bit later because I have a lie in but you'll find I'm there.' I let my eyes trait down her body when I say that so she can get an idea what I am on about. It is all highly polished stuff.

'My current milkman is rather unreliable,' says the bird. 'I never know when he's going to come.' She half opens her mouth and makes a small huffing noise. Percy trembles on the brink of a new love affair. 'Perhaps you could service my needs?'

'I could try,' I say. 'When would you like me to start?'

'As soon as possible,' breathes the bird. 'Would tomorrow be too early? My name's Jenkins. Jennifer Jenkins. Forty-seven Hillview Crescent.'

The address goes into my brain like it has been stamped there with a branding iron. The bird has long silky hair that curls inwards and she smells nice. Her figure is slim but capable of supporting two pleasant swellings that decorate the front of her sweater. She smiles again and slides off her stool.

'I'll see you tomorrow then. Don't be surprised if I don't answer the bell immediately. I'll probably be in bed.'

She makes another pouting motion with her lips and goes out.

Phew. If that wasn't an invitation then I don't know what is. I reach out and finish her drink. I don't fancy gin much but it seems a shame to waste it. I expect she was a bit over-powered by the brute of my presence. One is inclined to forget that women can become just as flustered as oneself in the presence of a love object.

The next morning I put on a clean pair of Y-fronts and pour a generous sprinkling of Mum's lily of the valley over the vital parts. Let nobody say that Timothy Lea is not a stickler for the refinements. You could eat your dinner off my dick provided you had a blunt knife and fork. I have not slept well and the memory of Jennifer Jenkins has been much with me. It all seems too easy somehow. I know I am irresistible, but dollies don't usually lay it on the line with such an endearing economy of dicky birds.

I whip round my patch with the nervous sweat building up underneath my armpits – normally I am as dry as a teetotallers' banquet – and arrive at forty-seven Hill-view Crescent smack on the dot of half-past eleven. My action man kit is possessed of a nervous tingle and I hope that it is not going to play up – or down as is more often the case at moments of nervous tension. I ring the doorbell and listen to the sound of the chimes dying away in the distance. It is as quiet as a demonstration by the Noise Abatement Society. Typical, the bird was probably having me on. I knew it was too good to be true. Suddenly, a figure swims into sight through the coloured glass. The door opens with a crack as if it has been freshly painted and I am face to face with Jennifer. She is wearing a black negligee with a matching robe and her breasts glow with a translucent bloom like freshly-boiled dumplings.

'Ah,' she says, 'you've come. I was on the point of giving you up. Where's the milk?'

'Oh yes,' I feel myself blushing. 'It's on the float. What would you like?' What a stupid berk I am. I have completely forgotten about the milk.

'It doesn't matter,' she says. 'We'll sort that out later. Come in.'

'Oh – er. Yes.' I go through the door like I am in a dream and she closes it behind me.

'I didn't think you were going to come,' she says, all eager like.

'I didn't think you were going to be here,' I say. We smile at each other and suddenly it is *Love Story* all over again – I never knew why they got that Ryan O'Neill bloke in the first place. She moves towards me and I hold her in my arms like she has just scored England's winning goal in the next World Cup.

'Come upstairs,' she says. 'I want to show you the bedroom.'

'Great,' I say. I mean, words fail you at moments like that, don't they? I suppose it was inevitable that there had to be a bird somewhere who was absolutely bonkers about me. It's probably the same with everyone. How lucky that I should meet this one before my eightieth birthday. I would hate us to have had to get our kicks from making the wheels on our bathchairs rub together.

Jennifer takes my hand and I try not to run up the

stairs two at a time. What a slinky body she has. Slim shoulders, narrow waist, tulip bum, long legs. The last time I saw a bird like that I was dreaming.

'Here we are.' She gives me an encouraging smile – it isn't necessary and throws open a door. The bed is the first thing I see and the first thing I am looking for. It has been slept in and a copy of the *Sunday Times Business News* is opened on the crumpled sheets 'Sunday mornings are heaven with the newspapers, aren't they?' she says following my glance. 'Still I don't expect you get the chance to read in bed, poor sweet.'

She puts her hands on my shoulders and I pull her to me and match my mouth to the anticipatory tilt of her head. She tastes of toothpaste and Nescafe. I kiss her gratefully and drink in the scent of her perfume. She smells of class. The room is as light and airy as my heart and I slide my hands inside her robe and settle them on the tight water melon mounds of her back bumpers. The important thing is not to rush, though it is going to be difficult to make percy understand that. He is already clambering up the front of my Y-fronts like a fast-growing vine. Jennifer lowers her arms behind her and the robe slides off and crackles down on to the paper. I bring my hand to the front of my trousers and slip it under my apron. She stops me as I begin to pull down my zip.

'Not yet. I want you to kiss me all over.'

She sinks back on to the bed and reaches behind her to throw the paper on the floor. Her legs are hanging over the edge and the hem of her night gown rests across her white thighs just below where her fuzz begins. I sit down beside her and run my hand up the inside of one of her legs from the ankle. I do it slowly, extending my fingers when I get to the soft flesh of her thighs. She shivers and put her hand over mine. I hold it and pull up her nightdress so that the silky mound is exposed. She pauses and then sits up and pulls the nightdress over her head. Her breasts dangle temptingly and I lean forward and take one in my mouth. My fingers go between her legs but she pulls my hand away.

'One at a time,' she says. 'I like to concentrate on each sensation.' I trace a pattern round the growing nipple and then nuzzle into the cleavage between the two breasts. Jennifer presses her breasts against my cheeks and then revolves them as if she is rolling pastry. Percy is beginning to go spare and again I feel for the release mechanism on the front of my trousers. It is bad to keep a growing hampton cooped up during the mating season.

'Not yet,' she breathes. 'Go down on me – please!'

The way she says it you would have to have a heart of stone not to comply and if I have a fault it has ever been over generosity in the grumble mumble department. I know there are some blokes who don't fancy a mouthful of furburger but I am definitely not one of them – I mean, the birds enjoy it so much, don't they? The dividend in human pleasure bestowed is well worth the crick in the neck and fag of picking the pubic hairs out of your teds.

Jennifer sinks back against the bed and her soft grey eyes look up at me pleadingly. Her long hair frames her face and her half-open mouth glistens temptingly. Reaching behind me I swiftly whip off one of my shoes and a sock and lie her longways so that her feet are pointing down the bed. I scramble on to the bed and raise one of her legs so that I lick the sole of her foot and insert my tongue into the gaps between her toes. She begins to respond and I bring my big toe into play against the entrance to her snatch. It is getting more slippery with every second and I slide my foot up and down the whole of the liquid length and press hard forcing back the lips and stubbing my big toe forward. It is an effective manoeuvre because of the difference in our heights.

'Go on!' I think I know what she is on about. Nothing is going to satisfy her until she feels the sharp, rasping end of my tongue darting against her clit.

I get off the bed and kneel beside it swinging Jennifer's legs round until my head is between them. Pulling her towards me I engage the inside of her thighs with my mouth and sweep my tongue up and down in a zigzag motion until my lips are brushing against the furry thicket. I take a few soft hairs in my mouth and pull gently. Jennifer purrs and then arches her back spontaneously as I run my tongue lightly along the thin pink line. I slide one arm round her thigh and open the willing flesh at the top of her dilly with two fingers spread wide. The skin is shell smooth and I dab at it with a butterfly touch of my tongue before probing for the clitoral cranny with a firm persistent pressure. Once I have established contact and can feel Jennifer beginning to churn, I move my fingers and with both hands begin to glide up the side aisles that surround the tunnel of love. Jennifer entwines her fingers in my hair and begins to buff my ears with her thighs.

It is at this moment that there is a loud crackling noise and I wonder if the bed has bust. I raise my head and see that the wardrobe door has sprung open to reveal a naked geezer trying to conceal an enormous hard. What I have heard described as conflicting emotions race through my system. The bloke is scarlet and I don't just mean the tip of his dongler.

'You swine!' he says. 'That's my wife!'

'I'm sorry.' I begin automatically. 'I had no idea you were married – I mean, she was married. I thought – ' and then it dawns on me. Why is this bloke hunched up in the cupboard?

It doesn't make sense. Unless – 'This is a put up job,' I say.

'You want me to put it up so you can get your rocks off. I've heard about this kind of thing.' I have too. Blokes who can't have it off unless they watch their old lady copping one from someone else.

'I'll get back in the cupboard,' says the bloke, completely changing his tune. 'We must fix that door, Jennifer.'

'Hang on a minute!' I say. 'I can't perform in these circumstances. It's not nice. I wouldn't be able to concentrate with you in there.'

'I'll sit by the bed,' says the bloke.

'That's even worse,' I say. 'Can't you push off to the pictures?'

'That's no good,' says the bloke. 'They do nothing for me. Go on with what you were doing. I liked that.'

'I liked it too,' says Jennifer.

'What do you mean, you liked it too?' says the bloke. 'You're not doing this for yourself, you know. You're doing it to prove how much you love me. You should be thinking of *me*.'

149

'Ah hem,' I say. 'I think I'd better be getting along.'

'You stay where you are,' says the bloke. 'You're in no position to do anything except what you're told. Creeping in to other people's houses and taking advantage of their wives. That's despicable.'

'I can't be taking advantage if she knows you're in there lapping it up,' I say 'I'm the bloke who's been taken advantage of.'

'Look,' says the bloke. 'This conversation is not getting us anywhere. I was coming along nicely until we started talking. Now look at me. Nothing.' He is right. His winkle had got a big crinkle in the middle of it and is melting away fast.

'I'm sorry,' I say. 'The magic has gone for me, too. I'd better go.'

Jennifer screws up her eyes and starts to sob loudly. 'I can't stand much more,' she sobs. 'There's not many wives who would put up with what I have to—the Mickey Mouse contraceptives, the wellington boots, the electrical gadgets. He tried to use one in the bath and nearly killed us both.'

'I wondered why your pubic hairs were straight,' I say.

'At least I care,' says the bloke. 'I may be bloody useless but I keep trying. A lot of people would give up and watch the telly.'

'I do wish you could be one of them,' says Jennifer.

'It's only a phase I'm going through, I'm certain of that,' says the bloke. 'It happens to lots of men. I expect it's happened to you?'

'It's happening at the moment,' I say. 'Now, for gawd's sake, let's pack this whole thing in. I couldn't bring myself to give your old lady one in the present circumstances. You need someone devoid of all human feeling.' A thought occurs to me. 'I'll have a word with my brother-in-law when I get back to the depot. Sidney Noggett, that's who you need. He's a nice – '

'Stay where you are!' barks Mr Jenkins. 'You come round here making my wife miserable and putting the mockers on my sex life and you expect to walk out of the front door as if nothing has happened. I'm not having it. Get your trousers off.'

'Oh Norman!' says Jennifer. 'You know I don't like that.'

'Don't like what?' I say. 'You mean, it's all right if I'm parting your pubics with my tongue but not with my old man?'

'I don't know where it's been,' she says.

'I can't give you a list,' I say. 'There's nothing wrong with it, I assure you. I've never had a dose of the coachman.'

'I'll get back in the cupboard,' says Norman. 'Just forget I'm here. Enjoy yourself.'

'Thank you, dear,' says Jennifer.

'Not *you*!' snaps Norman. 'Don't take advantage of my broadmindedness.' He starts to close the cupboard door on himself and then sniffs and sticks his head round it. 'And do go easy on the moth balls.'

'I was trying to kill him,' mutters the bird. 'Oh dear, this is so silly, isn't it.'

'You've broken my heart,' I say. 'I thought you really fancied me.'

'I do,' says the bird. 'I was really enjoying what you

were doing before he fell out of the cupboard.' She lowers her voice and whispers in my ear. 'I'd forgotten all about him. Come on, do it again.'

'Not unless I can go the whole way,' I say. 'I've been used enough for one morning.'

'All right,' she says. 'But you'll have to be quick. He won't like it once you start.'

'Can't we lock him in the wardrobe?' I say.

'There isn't a lock on the outside.' She comes into my arms again and this time does nothing to stop me undoing my belt. I quickly strip off my dicky dirt and nearly jump out of my trousers and pants. Now I am only wearing one sock. I might as well keep that on for Norman's benefit. It will probably add something as far as he is concerned. My mad mick is in an uncertain mood and curves doubtfully towards the floor but a brisk hand shake from Jennifer sends it lumbering into the vertical. She rubs it against her belly like it is a windscreen wiper attached to her fuzz and once again I taste those soft, pink lips. However, it is the other set that is closer to Mrs Jenkins's mind.

'Down, boy,' she murmurs. 'Just a little more and then you can put it in.'

She closes her eyes and programmes her face for ecstasy and I obediently glide my mouth down towards the quivering spasm chasm. Much as I have the lady's interest at heart I am reckoning on a quick binge on the minge and then the speedy introduction of the full frontal. It may be better to give than to receive but there is no point in being ridiculous about it. The damp curls tickle my hooter and I can feel percy lunging under the bed like a house detective. I take the soft frond of flesh that presents itself between my lips and – the wardrobe door bursts open behind me.

'Right! You dirty swine. That's enough.' I look up to see Mr Jenkins advancing upon me. He is gripping his hampton like he has just been given it for Christmas. It does not escape my attention that it is in a state of rude good health.

'Come on! Out of it! You've done your bit.' Opinions tend to differ on this last point and I shrug Jenkins aside and attempt to spear the funny clam. Hardly has my knob tasted paradise than Jenkins hurls himself at me and pushes me to the floor. Something snaps. A Lea can take so much and then – POW! Look out! As Jenkins turns towards his old lady I catch him a swinging blow on the side of the earhole and then follow this up with a bionic man right cross that stacks his features like the folds in a concertina. He staggers back across the room and collapses into the wardrobe. He clutches vainly at the clothes, bringing half of them down with him, and then slumps back, out to the world.

'Blimey!' I say. 'Do you think he's all right?'

'He will be for five minutes,' says Jennifer lying back and drawing up her legs temptingly. 'Come on. We've got some unfinished business to attend to.'

CHAPTER ELEVEN

In which Timmy and Sid take Daisy to the Festival of Milk.

'Well done, Lea. You've got the best stand at the show.'

'Thank you, Mr Claygate,' I say modestly.

'And I believe you put it up yourself?'

'I had a bit of help from Noggett,' I say.

Claygate's face clouds over. 'Ah, yes. Noggett,' he says. 'Somebody told me he's been going round selling home barbecue sets.' We are at the Festival of Milk which has been incorporated into the Smithfield Livestock Show. The stand referred to is that representing Meadowfresh and I have laboured long and hard on it. 'And the raffle tickets for the champion bull. I talked to the owners and they knew nothing about it.'

'I expect there's been some mistake,' I say. 'Noggett is very keen but he gets carried away sometimes.'

'You'll have to watch him,' says Claygate. He sees the look of awakening interest in my eye and pats my arm reassuringly.

'Yes, Lea. I've had my eye on you for some time and I think you're ready to take on more responsibilities. This firm is too big for one man to run and it's going to get bigger. I need men I can trust. Men of judgement. Men who can get on with the job and enthuse others. Men who combine humble reticence with diligence, dedication and discernment.'

'And that's me?' I say.

'I think so,' says Claygate. 'Originally I thought that Noggett was going to be my man but now I'm not so sure. There's something about him that – well, I find it difficult to quite put my finger on it.'

'I know what you mean,' I say. 'If you didn't know him you would think he was an unreliable layabout who was always on the fiddle. And if you did know him – ' my voice dies away helplessly.

'Precisely,' says Claygate. 'We will talk about this again later in the afternoon. A glowing future lies before you, my boy.' He gives me another pat and goes on his way. Success at last! And not before time. And all the sweeter because somebody has at last got Sid's number.

'Ah, there you are,' The irritable voice belongs to Sue who is wearing her milkmaid costume and a sulky expression. You will recall that I am to be her sponsor in 'The Milkmaid of the Year' competition.

'You look great,' I say. 'Like Little Bo Peep. All you need is a crook.'

This is the perfect cue for Sid to roll up which he does. 'Bloody heck,' he says. 'It's blooming difficult to sell these farmers anything. I suppose it's because they're used to getting it all free from the Government – hello, darling. Where's your sheep?'

'Don't you start,' moans Sue. 'I'd never have gone in for the contest if I'd known I had to dress up like this and answer questions on liver fluke. I thought I was going to be in a bathing costume.'

'That wouldn't be fair to the others,' says Sid. 'Knockout bird like you in a bathing costume. No contest.'

'Do you think so?' says Sue.

Something in her voice makes me scent danger. 'We'd better be getting round to the—' I begin.

'Do I look like a liar?' says Sid. 'Be reasonable – do I? I'm telling you exactly what I feel. I'm speaking from the heart. As far as I am concerned you are stunningly lovely. Everything about you beggars description. You are positively the most beautiful woman I have ever seen. The fact that I have gone through nearly thirty years of my life without setting eyes on you turns each one of them into a barren desert. To know that you walk the same planet will give a meaning to the rest of my life.'

'Sid—!' I say.

'Shut up!' says Sue. She takes Sid's arm and together they walk through to the back of the stand where we keep Daisy's hay. Daisy is another cow, but this time with four legs and a couple of horns. She is the living symbol of Meadowfresh that I have introduced from the residential course. Not the bleeder that trapped me in the loft but one specially chosen for its docility and – I find later – for passing its own weight in turds every couple of hours. Anyway, Claygate thinks it is a great idea which is the main thing and I shovel the Tom Tit on to the flowers outside the Farmers' Fertilizer stand next door when no one is looking. They are probably surprised that they don't get more visitors.

Oh dear, what am I going to do? I need Sue and Sid falling in love like a connecting tunnel between my ears. She is supposed to be on stage in fifteen minutes in the company of my fair self.

'Please don't do that, Daisy,' I say. 'I know you like

me.' She is getting a bit restless and has already eaten three hundred leaflets and a plastic watering can. 'Stay where you are,' I say soothingly. 'Daddy will be back in a minute.' I nip through the back flap and find my worst fears realized. Sid and Sue have already sunk down on a bale of straw and he has got her knockers out. It must be serious because he has taken off his tray of Everlast Drinking Straws – diced up lengths of indifferently patched inner tubing.

'Sue!' I hiss. 'What would Ellen say? Do your bodice up! You know how long it took to get that string threaded.'

'Piss off,' says Sid. 'Can't you find the grace to sling your hook in the presence of such an obvious act of spontaneous mutual adoration?'

It is obvious all right. Sue's face is flushed and sweaty and her eyes are glazed. I know the signs well – well, fairly well. She is lost with all hands – or at least the ones belonging to Sid. They are swarming all over her like a pawnbroker rearranging his window whilst all she can do is sigh and pant. How typical that after all my consideration and restraint I should get lumbered like this.

'Sid!' I shrill. 'Surely I can appeal to you?'

'You haven't been able to do so yet,' says the odious berk. 'Push us over that bale of straw, will you?'

Sue is playing lucky dips down the front of his trousers and it is clear that full intercourse is only seconds away. Perhaps I should get Mr Claygate? But no, after all the nice things he said he will expect me to deal with this kind of situation by myself.

'Sue!' I say. 'We're on stage in a couple of minutes.'

158

The wanton slut reaches up and paws at the front of my trousers. 'Come and join us,' she husks.

I am about to remonstrate with her – it's all right, it doesn't affect your eyesight – when it occurs to me that this may not be such a bad idea. If I can speed things up a bit then I may stand a chance of getting her back in the milkmaid costume she is just pulling over her head. Sid does not seem very keen to share his good fortune but I am not in the mood to put up with any more nonsense from him. I take my jacket off, hang my trousers over a bail of straw and swiftly apply myself to an aperture that Sid has left unoccupied – he is counting Sue's fillings with his hampton. At last, inside Sue Dangerfield and loving every moment of it. It couldn't happen to a nicer bloke, especially after all the trials and tribulations. I rest my hands on Sid's shoulders and belt out the love thrusts. No point in hanging around. The sooner I can bring us both off the better – I am, of course, referring to Sue and myself. Sid can make his own arrangements. Ooooooh! Here it comes. That lovely, tidal wave of soft, churning warmth fanning out through my – BANG! I nearly jump out of Sue's skin as the canvas wall of the stand splits open and is pulled over our heads. I look round past the crowds of gaping people and see that Daisy is contentedly grazing on the flowers outside the Farmers' Fertilizer Stand. It was clearly a mistake to tether her to the central pole of our stand.

Mr Claygate is looking down on us in the company of a party of senior officials from the Milk Marketing Board and the expression on his face might best be described as troubled.

159

'Right,' I say, addressing the surrounding crowd and trying to get a perky lilt into my voice. 'Thank you, Miss Prendergast. The next demonstration of artificial respiration techniques will take place at sixteen hundred hours.'